The Passion Of Ry Collier Infused Her With A Heated Desire.

Certainly physical desire. But mere infatuation? No matter how much she denied it, things had moved far beyond mere infatuation. Once again she was losing her heart to someone in spite of her intentions never to do it again. Then all her thoughts stopped and she gave herself over to the exhilaration building inside her.

Tonight, following the rehearsal dinner…

The decision to make love with him would take them down an unknown path, one that could lead to love or disaster. An uneasiness tried to replace the positive feeling. She shoved it aside. If she was falling in love—

If… That was a laugh. She knew in her heart that it had gone beyond the "if" stage. She was far too involved to turn back now.

Dear Reader,

Thanks for choosing Silhouette Desire, *the* place to find
passionate, powerful and provocative love stories. We're
starting off the month in style with Diana Palmer's
Man in Control, a LONG, TALL TEXANS story and the
author's 100th book! Congratulations, Diana, and thank
you so much for each and every one of your wonderful
stories.

Our continuing series DYNASTIES: THE BARONES is
back this month with Anne Marie Winston's thrilling tale
Born To Be Wild. And Cindy Gerard gives us a fabulous
story about a woman who finds romance at her best friend's
wedding, in *Tempting the Tycoon*. Weddings seem to be the
place to meet a romantic partner (note to self: get invited
to more weddings), as we find in Shawna Delacorte's
Having the Best Man's Baby.

Also this month, Kathie DeNosky is back with
another title in her ongoing ranching series—don't
miss *Lonetree Ranchers: Morgan* and watch for
the final story in this trilogy coming in December.
Finally, welcome back the wonderful Emilie Rose with
Cowboy's Million-Dollar Secret, a fantastic story about
a man who inherits much more than he ever expected.

More passion to you!

Melissa Jeglinski

Melissa Jeglinski
Senior Editor
Silhouette Desire

Please address questions and book requests to:
Silhouette Reader Service
U.S.: 3010 Walden Ave., P.O. Box 1325, Buffalo, NY 14269
Canadian: P.O. Box 609, Fort Erie, Ont. L2A 5X3

Having the Best Man's Baby

SHAWNA DELACORTE

Published by Silhouette Books

America's Publisher of Contemporary Romance

SILHOUETTE BOOKS

ISBN 0-373-76541-X

HAVING THE BEST MAN'S BABY

Visit Silhouette at www.eHarlequin.com

Printed in U.S.A.

SHAWNA DELACORTE

Although award-winning author Shawna Delacorte has lived most of her life in Los Angeles and has a background working in television production, she is currently living in Wichita, Kansas. She is honored to include among her writing accomplishments her placement on the *USA TODAY* bestseller list. In addition to writing full-time, she teaches a fiction-writing class in the Division of Continuing Education at Wichita State University. Shawna enjoys hearing from her readers and can be reached at 6505 E. Central, Box #300, Wichita, KS 67206. You may also visit her at her author page at the Harlequin Web site—www.eHarlequin.com.

To Margaret and Mike:
Thank you for the fun and the photography
And all your generosity.

One

———

Jean Summerfield froze in her tracks. Her breath caught in her throat. She spotted him as soon as she entered the private banquet room of the hotel. Her gaze remained riveted on the one face among those in the crowd that sent a shockwave of anxiety crashing through her reality. Painful memories from the past immediately shoved to the forefront. Her heart leaped into her throat and her mouth went dry. It couldn't be…not Ryland Collier… not after all these years. Ry Collier…the boy who had humiliated her and broken her heart fifteen years ago.

"Are you all right, Jean? You look like you've seen a ghost."

Jean turned at the sound of her best friend Susan Brundage's voice. "I…uh…yes, I'm fine. I thought I saw someone I knew from a long time ago, but I'm sure I was mistaken."

She glanced toward Ry again. Her stomach knotted into an uncomfortable ball. Her throat tightened. She thought she had put the past behind her, but in a fraction of a second all the insecurities suffered by that plain, overweight and shy sixteen-year-old girl came rushing back at her.

Susan grabbed Jean's arm, pulling her out of her thoughts. "There's someone you need to meet. He arrived from Chicago just this afternoon." Susan let out a soft chuckle. "He's what every woman's mother always warned her about…a bad boy with looks, charm and lots of money. A dangerous combination for sure. And guess what…he's single."

The knot in Jean's stomach tightened as Susan dragged her across the room toward the man she thought she would never see again. She took a calming breath, but it didn't help. She steeled her nerves against the inevitable, not sure what to expect.

"Ry, I'd like to introduce my maid of honor, Jean Summerfield. Jean, this is Bill's best man, Ry Collier. The two of you need to get acquainted. You'll be seeing a lot of each other during the upcoming week between now and the wedding."

A sexy smile lit Ry's handsomely chiseled features and a devilish gleam sparkled in his silver eyes as he made an obvious visual inventory of Jean's physical assets. He extended his hand toward her. "Jean, it's a pleasure to meet you." His smooth masculine voice tickled her senses as he clasped her hand in his, sending an immediate rush of sensual warmth through her body.

She reluctantly worked her hand out of his grasp, breaking the all-too-tempting sizzle of energy created by his touch. He was even more handsome up close than he had been from across the room. A sense of relief settled over her when he showed no outward signs of recognizing her. Perhaps the pain and emotional trauma of the past would remain safely tucked away.

Jean composed herself and her thoughts as she returned his smile. "The pleasure is all mine."

"Really?" He winked at her and flashed an absolutely killer smile. "We'll have to discuss mutual pleasure in greater detail..." He cocked his head and extended a questioning look. "Perhaps on the dance floor?"

Ry grasped her hand again, led her to the dance floor and pulled her into his arms. She hadn't shown any signs of recognizing him, but somewhere...somehow...their paths had crossed. He was sure of it, yet they couldn't possibly have met. He never would have forgotten this gorgeous woman with glossy chestnut hair, beautiful hazel eyes and a figure that could not be hidden by the businesslike tailored slacks and blazer she wore. It was a body that would fulfill any man's wildest fantasies.

A tightness pulled across his chest, an unwelcome sign saying that this woman represented far more than some sort of temporary casual association. A nagging sensation continued to pull at his senses telling him he knew her from somewhere...from someplace in his past. But where? A little twinge of uncertainty tugged at him followed by an ominous tremor of apprehension whose origins he didn't understand. Yes, indeed. She had definitely grabbed his libido. Now, if only he could figure out where he had seen her.

A shortness of breath caught him off guard when the delicate fragrance of her perfume tickled his senses. Just having her in his arms as they danced made his blood rush harder and his pulse race a little faster. Something about her had solidly grabbed his attention, pulled at his libido and made him want much more than just to hold her while they danced at a party.

Ry pulled her a little closer, taking advantage of the fact that she was already in his arms. He judged her height to be about five feet six inches, perfect for his six-foot height. He lowered his voice to a sexy whisper. "I know the bride is always supposed to be the center of attention, but you're certainly the most beautiful woman in the room."

The crimson flush of embarrassment quickly spread across Jean's cheeks as she glanced self-consciously around the room. "That's nonsense." A slight quaver surrounded her words, as if she wasn't sure exactly how to respond to what he had said. "Susan is a very beautiful woman. That marvelous mane of honey-blond hair and her big blue eyes…she'll be a stunning bride."

"I'm more impressed with the maid of honor."

Her embarrassment seemed genuine to him, not a pretense. Was it possible that she didn't realize just how beautiful she was? That she was not accustomed to compliments? Or even pickup lines? What a welcome change from some of the vain women he had known whose primary concern was how they looked on the outside without a thought to whether they were beautiful on the inside.

As they moved to the music, his mind drifted back fifteen years. He had known a girl in high school whom he liked very much. She was a beautiful soul on the inside and the one person he truly felt comfortable around…someone he could really talk with. He hadn't meant to, but he had destroyed that friendship as surely as if he had told her he never wanted to see her again. And for fifteen years the guilt and anguish had lived inside him.

Ry shook away the unpleasant memories and returned his attention to his very desirable dance partner. "This is a terrific idea...having a party so that everyone connected with the wedding can meet each other before the rehearsal and wedding ceremony. Have you known Bill and Susan very long?"

"I haven't known Bill that long. He moved to Seattle four years ago. Susan and I are both from Seattle and have lived here all our lives although we've only known each other for about eight years. We belong to the same little theater group. What about you and Bill? How long have you two known each other?"

"We went to college together at UCLA. We were roommates in our freshman year and have been close friends ever since. I moved from Los Angeles to Chicago about six months after I graduated. That's where my business is headquartered."

"What do you do for a living?"

"I have my own company. I analyze procedures and systems of companies, locate the waste of time and materials in the operation and make recommendations to streamline the business. I've just signed a contract for a four-week assignment here in Seattle that starts in a week, on the Monday after Sunday's wedding. How about you? What do you do other than belong to a little theater group and mesmerize unsuspecting men?"

Again the heat spread across her cheeks. "Please stop that. You're embarrassing me." She tried to regain her composure. She wasn't sure which bothered her more, the easy and empty flattery or the fact that it was Ry Collier saying the words. "I'm a personnel manager at a manufacturing company."

Ry pulled her even closer so that their bodies were pressed together as they danced. The last thing he wanted to do was discuss business with her. Every curve and angle of her body seemed to perfectly fit with his. The sexy fragrance of her perfume continued to assault his senses and stimulate his lustful desires. He wanted to nibble on her lips and kiss her delicious-looking mouth. And then he wanted to sweep her up in his arms, carry her off to the nearest bed and spend the rest of the night making passionate love to her.

He reluctantly returned his thoughts to the conversation at hand. He wasn't sure when or where, but with each passing minute he became more convinced that they had met somewhere. "I'm originally from Seattle." He watched her for any reaction to his words. He thought he felt her muscles tense slightly and her body stiffen for the briefest of moments. Was it his imagination?

She allowed her mind to wander as they moved to the music. It may have taken fifteen years, but she had finally ended up in Ry Collier's arms on a dance floor. His nearness was intoxicating. The pull of his sexy magnetism played havoc with her reality. Everything she had ever fantasized about him was happening at that moment. But it could not erase the hurt and humiliation of that night fifteen years ago. A sharp pang of sorrow hit her as the memories tried to crystallize in her mind.

"—have dinner with me tonight?"

Ry's words pulled her out of her thoughts. She furrowed her brow in confusion. "Dinner?"

"Let's say our goodbyes to Bill and Susan and find some quiet little restaurant where we can get better acquainted over dinner." He leaned his face very close to hers, his lips almost touching her ear. "Or better yet…we could go upstairs to my suite and order dinner from room service."

A surge of nervous energy shot through her body followed by a wave of apprehension. "So…you're, uh… you're staying at this hotel? That has to be pretty expensive for an extended stay."

"With several of the wedding functions planned to take place in this hotel, including the dinner after the rehearsal and the reception following the ceremony next weekend, this seemed like a good place to stay. I'll also be here through the duration of my four-week business contract after the wedding."

Five weeks? Her apprehension turned to anxiety. Could she be in contact with Ry for five weeks without her hurt and humiliation showing through? She tried to get her anxiety under control as she forced a tighter grip on her emotions. Just because he would be in town for that long didn't mean she would be having any contact with him past the reception following the wedding ceremony. His four-week work contract certainly wasn't anything where their paths would cross and they would find themselves in contact with each other.

The song ended and Ry escorted Jean from the dance floor. "Well? What about having dinner tonight?"

She had never felt so torn in her life. Should she tell him who she was or simply enjoy his attentions and pretend that the past didn't matter? "I just arrived. I think it would be rude for me to leave right away. After all, I am Susan's maid of honor. I should be here. And since you're the best man, I think that would apply to you, too."

He offered a sincere smile. "You're right, of course." He selected a small table in a quiet corner away from the dance floor and held out the chair for her. "What can I get you to drink?"

"A glass of white wine would be nice. Thank you."

He flashed his sexiest smile. "I'll be right back."

Ry headed for the bar. He was more convinced than ever that he knew the tantalizing Jean Summerfield from somewhere. Her smile, something about her eyes, the sound of her voice…wherever it was, he knew it was from long ago. Even though she pushed every lustful button he possessed, he associated her with something different and far more important, something warm and special…something he held very dear. If only he could place where and when.

He carried two glasses of wine back to the table, handing one of them to Jean before regaining his chair. He cocked his head and studied her for a moment.

Ry's unflinching gaze assailed Jean's senses as the discomfort over his continued stare grew inside her. She tried to force a casual and upbeat sound to her voice even though it was far from what she felt. "Is something wrong?" A nervous laugh escaped her throat. "Do I have dirt on my face?" She brought her hand to her cheek as if to brush away the offending smudge.

"Not at all." He captured her hand in his, holding it for a moment before letting it go. He lightly touched her cheek. "Your face is lovely."

A hint of irritation surrounded her words. She tried to hide her embarrassment. "Then why are you staring at me like that?"

"This may sound silly, but I have this weird feeling that we've met somewhere before. There's something about you that seems very familiar." He cocked his head. "Have we met before tonight?"

She weighed his question for a moment before answering. "I've never been to Los Angeles or Chicago."

A slight grin tugged at the corners of his mouth. "That's not really an answer, is it?" He eyed her curiously, his mind desperately trying to place her. "I lived in Seattle until I went to college. Perhaps when we were teenagers?"

She raised an eyebrow as she regarded the question that still lingered in his eyes. "Perhaps."

A slight frown wrinkled across his forehead as he stared intently at her. "Seriously...we have met somewhere, haven't we?"

"You tell me." The knot tightened in Jean's stomach again as an anxiety-ridden tremor worked its way through her body. He obviously intended to push at the topic until he got an answer that satisfied him. What if she told him they had never met? If he later discovered who she was, would he be upset? A little internal huff of disgust stopped her thoughts. He certainly didn't have any right to be upset fifteen years later. But still...it would be a blatant lie, which went against her grain.

Ry pushed forward with his desire to resolve his quandary. "Okay...I think we have met somewhere before. Since you say you've never been to Los Angeles or Chicago I'm going to assume we met when I lived in Seattle, rather than somewhere along the way with my travels."

He plumbed the depths of her eyes noting the uneasiness that belied her outer calm, an uneasiness that told him he had been right. But if she knew, then why was she refusing to tell him? It was a puzzling situation, something he had not come up against before and didn't know exactly how to handle. He lightly ran his fingertips across the back of her hand, then reached out and touched her cheek and hair. He once again relied on the charm that had gotten him through many an awkward moment. "Well, since you don't seem to want to tell me, let's tackle the dance floor again while I try to delve into my past and figure it out."

Once again Jean found herself in his arms moving to the music. Ryland Collier had been her dream and fantasy for the two years she knew him prior to the time he had embarrassed and humiliated her with the prom incident. And her nemesis for the fifteen years since then. She knew it was silly and ridiculous to hang on to the hurt of an adolescent happening for such a long time. She had managed to successfully put everything else from her high school days behind her—the dominance of the cold stern grandmother who raised her, insecurities about being overweight and having shabby clothes, embarrassment over the braces on her teeth and her ill-fitting glasses, her awkwardness and shyness around other people—but not her memory of that terrible night.

He brushed his lips lightly across hers, shocking Jean out of her thoughts. Then his words tickled in her ear. "Since we know each other from somewhere I thought a little 'hello again' kiss was in order." He pulled her closer. A teasing grin tugged at the corners of his mouth. "You wouldn't happen to be that little six-year-old girl who lived next door to me when I was seven, would you? The one I played doctor with?"

She couldn't stop the spontaneous laugh that followed his unexpected comments. "Definitely not. I didn't play doctor when I was a little girl."

His eyes sparkled with a teasing delight. "How about when you were a big girl?"

She tried to dismiss the excitement caused by the implication of his words. "I've never played doctor."

"It's not too late to learn." A bad boy grin tugged at the corners of his mouth. "I'll be happy to teach you the game."

He sounded more playful than threatening. Susan had been right—he was definitely a charmer. A little shiver of anticipation told her that playing doctor with Ry Collier would be an experience worth exploring.

The song ended. They returned to the table and what remained of their glasses of wine.

"You two getting along okay?" Bill Todd came up behind Ry, clamped his hand on Ry's shoulder and placed a quick kiss on Jean's cheek. "It wouldn't do for the best man and maid of honor to not be getting along."

It was Ry who immediately responded to Bill's question. "So far I've found out that Jean is a terrific dancer, wears very sexy perfume and never played doctor when she was a little girl." He flashed his patently charming smile, scooted his chair a little closer to hers and put his arm around her shoulder. "I told her I'd teach her how to play doctor tonight, but so far she's ignored my invitation. Other than that, we're getting along just fine."

Susan joined Bill, taking his hand in hers as she looked questioningly at Jean and Ry. "What's going on? Is everything okay?"

Jean detected the nervousness in Susan's voice and immediately moved to relieve her friend's tension. "Everything here is just fine, so stop worrying." She glanced around the room, then offered Susan a sincere smile. "Everyone is obviously having a great time."

Susan and Bill remained at the table for a few minutes, then moved on to greet some new arrivals. Jean watched as they walked away. "Susan is going to turn into a basket case if she doesn't calm down and stop worrying about every little thing."

Ry turned sideways in his chair until he faced her. "Is that the voice of experience speaking?"

"Are you asking if I've been the nervous bride?"

Ry glanced down at the table top, then regained eye contact with her. "Well...yes, I guess I am."

She paused for a moment as if she were contemplating his question. A frown marred her otherwise beautiful face. "Yes, I've been the nervous bride before. But for something that only lasted two years I could have saved myself the frustration."

He heard the bitterness in her voice and saw the discomfort dart across her face. "That doesn't sound like a very happy story."

"It isn't." She abruptly moved the conversation away from herself. "What about you?"

"Marriage? Not this confirmed bachelor." A bittersweet chuckle escaped his throat. "I don't even like to get too close to rice."

"So, you've never been married?"

"Once…very briefly…" A faraway look came into his eyes, followed by a deep-seated anger and bitterness that surrounded his words. "—a long time ago."

It was definitely a time in his life that Ry didn't want to talk about. He had been deceived, lied to and manipulated into a loveless marriage that never should have been. It was an experience he swore he'd never repeat. He tried to shove the bad memories away. He didn't want to think about that miserable time in his past, the two brief months of his marriage that seemed like two centuries.

He had better things to occupy his mind. He had set a goal for himself to be worth twenty million dollars by the time he was thirty-five. Through lots of hard work and shrewd investments he had almost reached his goal and he still had three years to go before his thirty-fifth birthday. He moved to change their conversation from the uncomfortable subject of marriage. He reached out and lightly touched Jean's cheek, then dropped his hand to cover hers as it rested on the table.

"Why don't you just tell me where we've met and save me the frustration of trying to figure it out?"

She drew in a steadying breath, then exhaled as she made her decision about what to say. An uneasy tremor grabbed her attention, telling her just how uncomfortable she found his insistence on an answer. But the topic had come to a point where she either had to create an awkward situation by telling him to drop it or confess their prior relationship. A lump formed in her throat. She attempted to swallow it before speaking. The nervous jitter that had been bouncing around inside her increased to an annoying distraction. Her words were somewhat tentative. She wasn't sure she really wanted to say them.

"Does the name Sally Jean Potter ring any bells with you?"

Ry couldn't have been more stunned if she had reached out and slapped him. He felt his eyes widen in shock. His words came out in a shaken whisper. "Sally Jean? You're Sally Jean Potter?"

He tried to talk, but only managed a sputtering attempt. "Sally Jean…I…" He shook his head as he tried without much success to say something intelligible. "I…you…"

The horrible guilt he had buried inside him fifteen years ago exploded into his consciousness. He had done a terrible thing to her, but at the time he believed there was no other choice open to him. The worst thing he had done was never explain to her what had happened, why he had canceled their prom date at the last minute. Canceled…perhaps stood up would be a more accurate choice of words. And now every sense and nerve ending in his body screamed at him to get out before things got worse. But how could it possibly be worse than it already was? Besides, he wasn't seventeen years old anymore.

He was a responsible adult who needed to face up to his past. He gathered his composure and tried his best to salvage the moment.

He forced a smile. "Sally Jean…I certainly didn't recognize you. You've changed quite a bit from high school." He reached out a slightly trembling hand toward her face, almost touching her cheek but stopping before he made physical contact. "No glasses, the braces are gone…"

"And I'm sure you can't overlook the fact that I've lost about thirty pounds."

He ignored the sarcasm in her voice. "That's quite a profound change from fifteen years ago."

Her defensive wall rose to combat her painful memories. Her harsh words carried an edge to them. "Yes, I agree… I was certainly an unattractive awkward mess of a girl back then."

Her response cut into him, leaving a definite wound and telling him just how much he had hurt her even though it had not been his intention. He cupped her chin in his hand and looked into the depths of her eyes. He leaned forward and quickly brushed his lips against hers. His words came out soft, but heartfelt and sincere. "That's not what I said. I never thought of you as an unattractive, awkward mess. I always thought of you as someone with special inner qualities that others didn't have and couldn't see."

It was not at all what Jean had expected him to say. She tried to assimilate his words into her anxiety, but they refused to mesh. Was he attempting to charm her out of an embarrassing moment or was he being honest? As much as she wanted to believe what he'd said, she didn't know if she could trust him.

Ry withdrew his hand and picked up his wineglass,

taking a sip before speaking. "When did you decide to drop the Sally and go by Jean?"

"Immediately after my divorce. At the same time that I started wearing contact lenses and lost the thirty pounds."

"Well...Sally Jean—"

"Just Jean if you don't mind." She heard the hard edge that continued to cling to her words even though she hadn't meant for it to be there. He hadn't said a word about what happened. Could he have forgotten all about the prom? Perhaps fate had worked in her favor this time by bringing her back in contact with Ry Collier so that the crushing experience could finally be closed and put to rest.

"Of course...Jean." He tried to force down the anxiety welling inside him. What possible purpose could be served by resurrecting a fifteen-year-old disaster? He was already carrying enough guilt to last two lifetimes without adding to it. He closed his eyes for a moment and an image of sixteen-year-old Sally Jean standing in the grocery store looking at him with pain-filled eyes just two hours after his last minute phone call to tell her he was sick and couldn't take her to the prom immediately popped into his mind. His throat tightened and a dull thud began to form at his temples. He shook the distressing image away and tried to shove the thought from his mind.

He fell back on the old reliable...his sexy smile and charm, although he wasn't feeling very charming on the inside. "You'll have to tell me what you've been doing since high school, catch me up on what's been happening in your life."

He twisted the stem of his wineglass between his thumb and fingers. "But first...I see your glass is empty, too. I'll get us another glass of wine, then we can have a long talk.''

''I don't need another—''

He picked up her glass, winked at her and flashed his most confident smile. ''I'll be right back.''

Jean watched as he made his way through the assembled guests to reach the bar. She turned away, closed her eyes and tried to calm her shattered nerves. Anxiety churned in the pit of her stomach. Ry Collier was everything any woman could want, at least he was everything she had ever wanted. He had never been far from her thoughts all through college, during her short-lived marriage, the disastrous relationship that followed her divorce and the years since.

A moment later Ry returned with two filled glasses. He handed her a glass, then sat down. He raised his glass toward her in the form of a toast. ''Here's to old friends and getting reacquainted.''

Jean took a sip from her glass, then set it on the table. She ran her index finger around the rim. Her words came out almost as if she had not intended to say them out loud. ''Old friends…getting reacquainted…that covers a lot of territory, a lot of time and a lot of water under the bridge.''

An uncomfortable sensation pulsed through Ry's body raising his anxiety level a couple of notches. His high school days were a place and time in his life that he didn't really want to discuss, return to or delve into anew. Every time someone contacted him about attending his high school reunion—five years, ten years and then just that summer the fifteen-year reunion—he had made it very clear that he was not interested. He had worked hard over the years overcoming the circumstances of his childhood and youth in order to achieve the success he enjoyed today. He didn't want to relive those bad times.

Sally Jean had been his only haven back then. He could be himself with her and didn't have to constantly be on guard to make sure he didn't let that facade slip. He had valued their friendship above all others. And he was the one who had destroyed it. Now fate had given him the opportunity to fix the sins of the past, only he hadn't been prepared for that past to hit him so abruptly. For someone who was always confident in his words and actions, he wasn't sure exactly how to go about handling this.

He covered her hand with his. "Let's see if we can't lessen the territory, shorten the time and get rid of some of that water flowing under that bridge."

Once again his nearness made her heart pound and her pulse race. His touch sent tremors of excitement through her body. As much as she wanted to maintain an emotional distance from him, every breath she took seemed to pull her farther and farther into his realm. She steeled herself against his magnetic pull. Before anything else, though, she needed to know what had happened fifteen years ago. She had to put closure to the pain she had been carrying for all those years. She shifted her weight in her chair, fully aware of how awkward it appeared.

Jean's discomfort was not lost on Ry. He glanced at his watch. The time startled him back to the reality of his business world. He was torn between his responsibilities and his personal needs. He didn't want to walk out on her at such an inappropriate moment, but he had pressing business matters that required his attention.

"I didn't realize it was so late. I have a business associate who's expecting a phone call from me. I need to be on my way."

"Oh?" The skepticism in her voice matched the uncertainty pushing at her consciousness, an uncertainty
mixed with her surprise at his sudden need to leave and
disappointment over his apparent decision to turn and
run rather than address the past. "Does this mean that
your invitation for dinner tonight was nothing more than
a come-on line? Just idle conversation? Now that you
remember me, you have something else that needs your
immediate attention?"

Once again her words cut through directly to his deep-
seated guilt. He placed his hands on her shoulders. His
voice was filled with sincerity, his words soft. "Not at
all. If you had accepted my dinner invitation I would
have immediately rearranged my business schedule. Un-
fortunately, it's now a little too late to do it."

He framed her face with his hands, peered intently into
her hazel eyes, then leaned forward and once again
brushed his lips gently against hers, the kiss lingering a
little longer than last time. "Have dinner with me tomorrow night. We'll go to a nice restaurant overlooking
the water."

He saw the hesitation in her eyes and took steps to
stop her before she could say no. "I'll pick you up at
six o'clock tomorrow evening. What's your address?"

"No... I can't agree to have dinner with you."

"No? Why not?"

"Not until I know..." It was more than she had anticipated saying. She wished she hadn't started any of
this. The circumstances had moved like lightning until
they were beyond what she had imagined and now it
was too late to take any of it back. The trepidation welled
inside her sending a nervous jitter through her body. She
knew the arguments. It was stupid to still be carrying the
emotional baggage of that teenage girl fifteen years later,

especially with all the other unhappy twists and turns her life had taken since that time. It was ridiculous to allow it to linger in her consciousness and to dwell on it. But the pain and sense of betrayal had been so great that even after all these years it refused to go away.

She knew it would open old wounds and subject her to the hurt all over again, but she had to know what happened and why. Her throat went dry and her mouth felt as if it was stuffed with cotton. The shattered emotions of that sixteen-year-old girl tried to take control. She managed to force out the words, her voice not as firm and confident as she wanted it to be.

"I need to know, Ry. I need to know what happened fifteen years ago. Why did you lie to me about being sick? Why did you stand me up for the prom? Why would you do such a terrible, hurtful thing? Why would you purposely humiliate me like that?" She squirmed uncomfortably in her chair. He seemed to be staring at her, yet his eyes had the look of someone who was a million miles away.

Was he even listening to her? Was the entire event so insignificant and unimportant to him that he didn't even remember it? A tremor of anxiety told her that perhaps she had been wrong in pressing him for an explanation. Each passing second of silence sent an additional ripple of trepidation through her consciousness.

Two

Ry's silence left Jean uncomfortable. She felt compelled to say something—anything to break the ominous quiet. "You certainly led a charmed life back then—captain of the football team, senior class president, voted most popular boy in school. You had the world in the palm of your hand. You had it all."

She quickly swallowed the sob that tried to force its way out of her throat. "With all of that, why did you feel that you needed to play such a cruel joke on me? Why?"

A quick look of despair flashed across his handsome features. Sarcasm filled his voice and surrounded his words. "Yeah, I had the world in the palm of my hand. I had all that and more, such as needing to be what people wanted me to be, having to fit in with their expectations of who I was…pretending to live each day as if I didn't have a care in the world." A bittersweet chuckle passed through his lips. "A truly charmed life."

He furrowed his brow in momentary concentration as if trying to gather his thoughts. His words contained an undeniable emotion touched with a genuine sadness. "You were the only person I felt comfortable with, the only one where I could be myself and not hide behind a facade. You were the only one I could really talk to."

His words caught her totally off guard. They were the last thing she expected to hear from him. Had she been so wrapped up in her own problems that she had failed to notice what had been happening with him back then? Had she failed to notice a friend who was quietly reaching out to her?

She forced down her apprehension and tried to keep her own pain out of her voice, but a small sob caught in her throat as she started to speak. "I have to know… fifteen years ago, Ry…what happened that night? I was thrilled when you asked me to the prom. I had never been happier in my entire life. I was floating on air from the moment you invited me. Then just an hour before you were supposed to pick me up you called and said you were sick. I was crushed, but I understood. Then two hours later I saw you at the grocery store looking perfectly healthy and fit. I started to speak to you, but you turned away from me and hurried out the door. I had never been so devastated in my life. I went from the highest of highs to the lowest of lows in just a few hours."

Another sob formed in her throat and she fought to keep it out of her voice. "And then Monday at school you ignored me completely. It was as if you couldn't get away from me fast enough. What happened, Ry? I thought we were friends. Was it your idea of a joke? If so, it was a horribly cruel one.''

The pain she had been desperately trying to keep at bay finally exploded inside her as fresh and penetrating as it had been that night fifteen years ago. ''What could I possibly have done that caused you to treat me that way? Why did you betray me like that?''

Ry squirmed uncomfortably in the seat. Anger and hurt were emotions he understood thanks to his father. Even the experience of humiliation. But betrayal? That word cut through him like a sharp knife. It wasn't a word he had expected her to say. He could no longer ignore the situation or keep his own pain and guilt buried in an attempt to pretend it didn't exist. He had to bring it out into the open…to tell her the truth.

He took a calming breath. A touch of panic assaulted his consciousness. The easy charm he used so effectively had deserted him to be replaced by an uncertainty he had seldom experienced as an adult.

He reached out and took her hand becoming immediately aware of the way her muscles tensed, yet she did not pull away. He took a deep breath, then slowly exhaled as he tried to collect his thoughts.

''I've been carrying around a huge load of guilt about this for fifteen years, but I didn't think I'd ever have to talk about it. I'm not even sure exactly how to explain it.'' He paused for a moment to try to put things in some type of logical order before tackling what he hoped didn't sound too stupid.

''Let me start with some of my background, some things that I've never shared with anyone.'' He took another steadying breath. ''My father, to put it politely, was a shiftless bum and a gambler who couldn't be depended on for anything. His promises meant nothing. Whether he believed them when he made them, I don't know. What I do know is that he never kept any of them. He couldn't hold a job or properly provide for his family.''

A bittersweet chuckle escaped his throat. ''I'm sure that's where my compulsive drive for success came from.'' Other memories invaded his mind, painful times from a lot longer ago than the fifteen years they were talking about. ''I remember one particularly awful Christmas when I was eight years old. I wanted a train set. It was the only thing I wanted. One day about a week before Christmas I was in the apartment alone. I went snooping in the closets and found my Christmas present. There was only one gift with my name on it. I carefully unwrapped the package just enough to peek at the box inside. I was so excited when I saw that it was my train. I sealed the package shut and put it back where I'd found it. The excitement danced inside me to the point where it was all I could do to wait the one week until Christmas.

''On Christmas morning I rushed into the living room, but the package I had peeked at wasn't under the tree. Instead, there was a small package that was poorly wrapped with a little tag on it bearing my name, written in my father's handwriting. My beloved train set wasn't there. I didn't understand it that morning when I opened my one present and found underwear and two pairs of socks. I looked at my mother and saw the tears and sadness in her eyes even though she was trying to maintain an upbeat holiday spirit. All I saw on my father's face was indifference. It was yet another disappointment in a long line of many, but this one really hurt. It wasn't a matter of something promised, but not delivered. The train had been there. I had seen it. But by Christmas morning it had disappeared.

"That night after I'd gone to bed I heard my mother and father arguing. My father had taken my train set back to the store for a refund and then had lost most of the money gambling. I remember crying myself to sleep that night."

He shook the painful childhood memory from his mind. "Well, enough of the distant past. To return to your question about what happened the night of the prom. The reason I couldn't go was simply that I didn't have the money. What I'd saved to pay for my tux rental and to buy you a corsage all had to be used to help pay the rent that month. Dear ol' Dad promised to get the money back to me so I could take you to the prom. I had hoped against hope that this time it would be the truth even though deep down inside I knew it wasn't going to happen."

He looked into the depths of her eyes in an attempt to find some acceptance for his explanation, some measure of comfort. "I guess that's why I waited so long before I finally called to say I couldn't go. I kept telling myself that this would be the one time things would work out and he'd come through for me."

Ry allowed a sigh of resignation before continuing. "But, of course, Dad never came through with the money." He took the last swallow of wine from his glass. All the disappointment he had experienced that night fifteen years ago flooded through him. He looked up at Jean.

"And that's why I told you I was sick and couldn't go. I was too ashamed to tell you the truth. And when I saw you at the grocery store later that Saturday evening and then on Monday at school...saw the hurt and bewilderment on your face...I couldn't face it or you. I knew I had hurt you and I felt terrible and very guilty, but I didn't know what to do about it." He clenched his jaw into a hard line as he wrinkled his brow into a frown. "I swore that day that I'd never again allow myself to be in a position where I needed to depend on anyone else for anything."

The anxiety churned inside him. He was accustomed to being in control of situations and certainly of his own emotions. It had been many years since he felt such a lack of control over what was happening and it was a feeling he didn't like. He took Jean's hand in his, hoping it would calm his inner turmoil. "That's what happened fifteen years ago. I'm sure there must have been a better way of handling the situation, but at the time I just didn't know what else to do."

He placed his fingertips beneath her chin and lifted until he could look into her hazel eyes. "I never meant to hurt you. Please believe me. That was the last thing I wanted. I'm sorry I couldn't tell you the truth then, but I was too ashamed and embarrassed. I didn't want anyone to know what life was like for me at home. I know it's asking a lot, especially after all these years, but will you please forgive me for treating you so badly?"

Jean sat in stunned silence for a moment before she could respond. What she had just heard was far removed from what she had anticipated. "I had no idea. In school you always seemed like you had everything—whatever you wanted seemed to automatically happen for you."

"I worked hard to create that image. That's why you were so important to me. You were the one person I felt comfortable around, the one person who I felt wasn't judging me or holding me up to impossible standards— the one person who was capable of accepting me for who I was rather than who you wanted me to be. Your friendship was very special to me, it was the single most im-

portant thing from my high school days. That's why I
wanted to take you to the prom.''

A calm began to descend over her, replacing the anxiety that had been churning in the pit of her stomach.
''Then why didn't you tell me the truth so I would have
known what happened?''

''I guess when you're a confused teenager some things
just don't come out logically,'' he said, shrugging his
shoulders.

''The next day I heard some of the cheerleaders talking in the gym locker room…'' Jean's voice trailed off
as once again the memory sent waves of humiliation
crashing through her. ''They were laughing and saying
you had only invited me as a joke.''

She saw a flash of anger dart through his eyes as he
clenched his jaw again. ''I hope you didn't believe what
they said. They were a vain, empty-headed group of
snobs and not one of them could measure up to you in
intelligence, compassion and just being a real person.
The entire group of them put together wouldn't have
made one worthwhile person who you would want as a
friend.''

She believed him. It was as if a huge weight had been
lifted from her shoulders. After all these years she finally
knew what had happened. She saw a hint of apprehension in the depth of his eyes, an anxiety that clouded the
silvery color to a soft gray. It was almost as if he desperately needed her verbal acceptance of his explanation.

She allowed a little bit of a smile to turn the corners
of her mouth. ''Thank you for sharing that with me. For
fifteen years it's been a twisting pain living inside me.''

''You haven't said anything about forgiving me for
my horrible behavior on prom night. I would really like

for you to lift this mantle of guilt I've been wearing all these years."

Jean looked up at him, at the emotion that turned his silver eyes to a cloudy gray, at the anxiety she found there. "Yes... I forgive the actions of a seventeen-year-old boy and I want to thank you for finally letting me know what really happened so I can put closure to that painful incident from my past."

He squeezed her hand, then brought it to his lips as the relief washed through his body. After fifteen years he had found his dear friend from high school and had resolved the guilt that had been part of those final weeks of his senior year and lingered on for the ensuing fifteen years.

A broad smile covered Ry's face. "Now, what about dinner tomorrow night? What's your address? Where do I pick you up?"

She whispered her address and the pleasure welled inside him. She was giving him a chance to repair their long-ago relationship and it was a chance he wouldn't waste. "I'll see you tomorrow evening." He glanced at his watch again. "Now I really need to take care of business." He gave her hand another squeeze, then hurried toward the door pausing a moment to look over his shoulder and wink at her.

Ry walked down the hallway, then took the elevator up to his suite. Even as he grabbed his day planner to look for the phone number of his client, his thoughts were on Jean and what had just happened between them. What started as a traumatic experience had ended on an up note. He had finally been able to unburden himself, to explain to someone who was very important to him exactly what had happened so many years ago. The pleasure tugged at the corners of his mouth, turning them upward into a smile. His dear friend from high school, Sally Jean, had forgiven him. And tomorrow they would be having dinner together—their first real date.

Jean nervously stared at the clock as it grew closer and closer to the time of Ry's arrival for their dinner date. She had dressed three times and each outfit had somehow seemed wrong. She finally settled on a royal blue knee-length chiffon cocktail dress. He had said they would be going somewhere nice and she wanted to make sure she was appropriately dressed.

The sound of the doorbell sent a wave of apprehension coursing through her. Even though she and Ry had settled the past, she was about to embark on a real date with her first love from her teenage years...an adult date, not an adolescent infatuation. It had been many years since she had been this nervous. She took a steadying breath, then a second one before rising from the chair.

She opened the door to a very handsome man wearing a charcoal-gray custom-tailored suit. Everything about him projected a sense of power and confidence. He looked rich, successful and incredibly desirable. She knew she should be saying or doing something, but all she could do was stare at the man who had been her fantasy for so many years.

"May I come in?"

Ry's words startled her out of her daze. "Oh...yes, of course." She stepped aside and motioned him in.

He looked around the tastefully decorated living room, which had a fireplace. He peered beyond to the dining room and kitchen. Then he glanced toward the stairs that he assumed led up to the bedroom.

"This is a lovely condo and you've certainly decorated it nicely. Did you do it yourself?"

"Thank you. Yes, I had to do it myself. There's no way I could have afforded a professional decorator."

"Do you prefer living in a condominium to having a house?"

"Yes, for right now. There's no yardwork with a condo and since I have a town house, I still have my own garage and can go directly from the garage to my kitchen without going outside. That's very convenient when it's raining."

A hint of anxiety began to churn in the pit of her stomach as she engaged in awkward small talk. Did he feel the same tension in the air as she did? She attempted to shove the disconcerting sensation aside before it grew any more uncomfortable.

"You didn't say where we were going for dinner so I wasn't sure exactly what to wear." She self-consciously glanced down at her dress. "I hope this will be okay."

His silver eyes sparkled with pleasure as he looked her up and down, then flashed a smile that seemed to be a combination of gentlemanly response and lustful desire. "You look beautiful." He took her hand in his and brought it to his lips, then continued to hold on to it. "I've made reservations for seven o'clock. Shall we go?"

The evening was everything Jean had fantasized it would be. Ry had eyes only for her. His witty conversation showed a great depth of knowledge as they discussed many different topics. They lingered over after-dinner coffee, then strolled hand in hand along the waterfront. The cool night air sent a shiver across her skin.

Ry removed his suit jacket. "Here, this should keep

you warm.'' He placed it around her shoulders, then they continued to stroll along the street hand in hand.

She snuggled into the warmth of the jacket. A hint of his aftershave clung to the fabric sending a tingle of anticipation through her senses. His touch thrilled her. His mere presence sent tremors of excitement through her body. She felt as if she was floating on a cloud made of hopes, dreams and expectations that touched every corner of her existence.

Jean's emotions raced into high gear. She had never spent a more glorious evening in her entire life. The adult Ryland Collier had lived up to everything she had ever fantasized about him. He was charming, attentive, a sparkling conversationalist and a surprisingly good listener. He treated her as if she was the only woman in the world and the most important person he knew. Everything he said and did made her feel very special.

And underlying it all sizzled an incredible sexual energy resonating from him. It reached out and grabbed her on the most primal of levels. Her senses tingled with desire, leaving her nearly breathless and wanting more. The sensations bordered on frightening in their magnitude and intensity. As they drove back to her condo all the thoughts and feelings of an enchanting evening swirled around in her head, creating a warm glow of contentment more potent than any she had ever experienced.

Ry pulled his car into her driveway and turned off the engine. He walked Jean to her porch, then took the key from her hand and unlocked the front door for her. She impulsively turned toward him and blurted out the words before she had time to think about them. ''Would you like to come in for a cup of coffee?''

He handed her the door key, his pleasure showing on his face. "Yes, I'd like that very much."

Jean quickly made some coffee, carried two filled mugs into the living room, and placed them on the coffee table. They settled into the couch.

He put his arm around her shoulder and pulled her close to his side. "I'm so glad we were able to put our past behind us. I said more than I intended to, though. I must apologize for boring you yesterday with that story about my train. It just slipped out." He placed a soft kiss on her forehead, then flashed a teasing smile. "Since you managed to get me to bare my soul to you last night, I think it would be fair if you took your turn."

In spite of his grin, she saw the honesty in his eyes, a truth that spoke to her of sharing. It connected with her own unhappy and lonely childhood. He had shared some of his painful memories with her. She felt drawn to do the same.

Her words came out softly, filled with an irony she had not anticipated. "Well, it turns out that we have more in common than just having gone to high school together."

"Oh? What else do we have in common?" Everything felt so natural. It was much like the sensation of closeness and friendship he had always experienced when he was around Sally Jean in high school—except now her perfume was driving him crazy, just touching her made his pulse race and seeing the beautiful woman she had become tugged at his lustful desires. But it wasn't all surface beauty. He had the privilege of knowing the truly beautiful person who lived inside her, too.

"A miserable home life when we were in school."

He cocked his head and shot her a questioning look. "Really? As long as we're getting reacquainted and revealing painful secrets, would you like to tell me about it?" A teasing grin pulled at the corners of his mouth. "I showed you mine, now I think it's your turn to show me yours…so to speak."

He saw her eyes widen in surprise. He gave her shoulder an encouraging squeeze. "Seriously, I'm a good listener if you'd like to tell me about it."

Once again he made her feel very special. She felt as if she could trust him with some of her past secrets. "I don't know if you were aware or not, but my parents died in a plane crash when I was ten years old. I lived with my grandmother, a harsh and cold woman who had been raised on a farm by strict parents who didn't hold with city ways or people who indulged in what they considered frivolous activities. I was so disappointed when you called to say you were sick and couldn't go to the prom and was totally devastated when I saw you at the store later that night. Instead of emotional support to help ease my pain, all I got from my grandmother was an 'I told you so…stay in your place…you're not a fancy girl who should be going to fancy parties.'

"And then Monday it was the cruel laughter from the cheerleaders…the same group of girls who always teased me about my weight and old clothes. They had simply reinforced what my grandmother had always made me feel—that I was unattractive, dull and didn't deserve any better than what I had and shouldn't strive for more. It took me years and lots of hard work to overcome all those old insecurities."

"I'm so sorry I put you through that. I'm also sorry that we weren't able to share our troubles back then when we could have helped each other." Ry leaned back and pulled her into his embrace. "Knowing you was the one bright spot of my high school days."

She couldn't stop the little laugh of surprise. "You mean being senior class president and captain of the football team weren't bright spots in your life?"

"They were the facade I was living with, not the bright spots." He placed a tender kiss on her cheek. "Even though you had an unhappy home life you certainly turned out well. You're as beautiful on the outside as you've always been on the inside."

The heat of embarrassment spread across her cheeks combining with the heat of desire that coursed through her veins. His words grabbed her much like an addictive drug. From the moment she had spotted Ry at the party the previous night her emotions had been on a roller coaster ride. But now it seemed that the ride had finally ended and she was safely back on firm ground.

Well, maybe safely wasn't exactly the right word. A tingle of apprehension, edged with just a hint of fear, darted through her body. After her marriage and then the horrible relationship that followed with what she thought was the perfect man, she swore she would never give her heart to anyone again. But the infatuation of sixteen-year-old Sally Jean for seventeen-year-old Ry had never quite gone away. As an adult, could she hope to be able to win the heart of Ryland Collier, a man who had professed to being a confirmed bachelor? Could she trust him not to take advantage of her delicate emotions and vulnerability where he was concerned?

Maybe the trauma of the past had been resolved, but what about the ensuing week when they would be thrown together on numerous occasions in an atmosphere surrounded by love and wedding preparations? A quick jolt of panic left her uncertain about what the outcome of their new association would be.

Jean glanced at the clock above the fireplace as she

rose from the couch. "Well, it's getting late. Even though tomorrow is Sunday, I have several things that I need to do first thing in the morning—some last-minute items I promised Susan I'd help her with. So, perhaps we'd better say good-night."

"It's been a lovely evening. Thank you for sharing it with me. I'm so glad we've had the opportunity to put the past behind us."

She glanced shyly at the floor. "Me, too."

"Well, I guess I'll be saying good night then." He started to pull her into his embrace.

Another surge of panic hit her. Was this the moment when he would be expecting a good night kiss? A real kiss and not just a simple brushing of lips? A nervous jitter darted through her body leaving her apprehensive and unsure. In spite of his confession from the past, were his attentions only his response to the new Jean, just as they had been at the party when Susan had introduced them and he had looked her over and flirted shamelessly before he knew who she was? Would he be interested in pursuing a passionate kiss if she were still the plain, overweight Sally Jean?

She took a step back, her anxiety causing her to impulsively stick out her hand to offer a handshake. "Thank you so much for a delightful dinner."

A visibly surprised Ry ignored her hand, pulled her into his embrace and captured her mouth with a passion-filled kiss that spoke directly to her of the sensuality that was Ryland Collier. The moment his lips touched hers, every inch of her body tingled with excitement. The kiss was everything she ever imagined it would be…and more. At that moment she didn't want him to ever let go of her.

Jean slipped her arms around Ry's neck. She ran her

fingers through his thick hair. Everything about him excited her more than she thought was possible. She had been totally unprepared for the amount of passion his kiss conveyed, a passion she returned without hesitation.

The earthiness of her kiss sent a wave of sensual energy burning through Ry that almost knocked him back on his heels. It was much more than what he had expected and even a little more than he had been prepared to handle at the moment. A surge of panic hit him when he realized the emotional impact attached to the kiss. It was a confusing mixture, the comfort and familiarity of a dear friend from the past combined with the incendiary temptation of a fascinating and sexy woman who pulled at every lustful desire he had ever harbored. It left him reeling without a clear direction.

He reluctantly broke off the kiss. He cradled her head against his shoulder as he tried to collect his thoughts and rein in his galloping libido. As much as he wanted to pursue the delectable Jean Summerfield, he did not want to take a chance on alienating Sally Jean Potter from his life again. He felt trapped in a no win situation.

He found his voice, but was not happy with the husky quality that surrounded his words. "It's getting late. I'll call you tomorrow afternoon. I have some work to do, a meeting and a few preliminary details to get out of the way before I start on my new work project. As far as the wedding activities are concerned, we have a dinner with Susan and Bill on Tuesday night, then there's the traditional bachelor party on Friday night, the rehearsal and rehearsal dinner on Saturday evening followed by the wedding on Sunday. Maybe we could squeeze in dinner and a movie among all those other activities? Perhaps tomorrow evening?"

Jean managed to force out some words that she hoped

weren't too incoherent, but she feared they sounded more like gibberish than her agreement to a movie. She walked Ry to the front door and watched as he climbed into his car and backed out of the driveway. As she closed the door she touched her fingers to her lips where the burning intensity of his kiss still lingered. Her pulse raced and her heart continued to pound. Ryland Collier was definitely a force to be reckoned with, a dynamic man with enough sexual magnetism to fill a room.

She closed her eyes and leaned back against the door. What would the future bring? Did she have a chance to capture the heart of this dynamic man? Would they be seeing each other after Susan and Bill's wedding was over?

A little scowl wrinkled across her forehead as a thought dampened her spirit. He had admitted to a brief marriage, but what had happened that would cause him to adamantly declare himself to be a confirmed bachelor? Was his marriage as miserable as hers had been? Did they have even more in common than an unhappy home life as a child? Whatever they had in common in the past, it certainly wasn't something that a future could be built on.

Jean shook her head to clear out the wandering thoughts that had started down a strange path, a path that seemed to materialize out of nowhere based on nothing more than a passionate kiss and memories of a teenage crush.

She walked upstairs to her bedroom. *Get a grip on yourself. You're being ridiculous. It was dinner and a kiss…nothing more.*

Somewhere in the back of her mind she knew she was lying to herself. It was more…a lot more. But was it more than she was prepared to handle? More than could ever be?

Three

Jean hurried home Sunday afternoon, rushing to her answering machine before even taking off her jacket. Her errands had taken longer than she anticipated and she feared she might have missed Ry's promised call. At first she was pleased to see that there were no messages. She had gotten home in time. Then another thought hit her. What if he wasn't going to call?

She tried to collect her scattered thoughts as she hung her jacket in the hall closet. After all, Ry had not said definitely about going to a movie and dinner. It had been left open, that he would call. Perhaps he had become involved in some kind of business meeting? She tried to shove her disappointment aside, but it told her just how attracted she was to Ry Collier and how much she wanted to see him again on a purely social basis having nothing to do with their wedding responsibilities as maid of honor and best man.

She glanced at her watch. It was two-thirty and she hadn't eaten anything since breakfast. She wandered listlessly toward the kitchen. Then the phone rang. She raced to answer it, her heart pounding with excitement. It had to be Ry.

"Hi. I waited to call to make sure you'd had enough time to take care of all your business matters."

As soon as she heard his voice a warm sensation washed through her. "Your timing is perfect. I've only been home for a couple of minutes."

"Are we still on for a movie this afternoon and then dinner?"

"Yes, that sounds great."

"Good. I'll pick you up in an hour. Why don't you check the movie listings and pick out a film you want to see and I'll make reservations for dinner?"

"Anything special you want to see?"

"Whatever you pick will be fine with me. I'll see you in a little while."

Jean paused for a moment, her hand lingering on the phone receiver after hanging up. A smile turned the corners of her mouth as she thought about her upcoming afternoon and evening with Ry. In fact, he had been all she thought about the entire morning. The smile faded and was quickly replaced with a slight frown. Was she becoming too enamored of Ry Collier? Was it too much too quickly?

She forced the thought away as she grabbed the newspaper to check the movie listings.

Following the movie Ry and Jean entered the restaurant, her hand clasped tightly in his. They were seated at a window table overlooking the ocean.

"That was a great movie. I don't know when I've laughed so much," Jean said, enthusiastically.

"Same here." He reached across the table and took her hand. His expression turned serious. "Thanks for sharing it with me. I'm glad you were able to take care of all your morning errands so that you were free this afternoon." He felt so comfortable with her, more so than any other person he had ever been with. Once again he flashed on the way he could be himself around her without any pretenses. In high school, he had to live up to an image. As a successful businessman, he needed to appease clients and be diplomatic in strained situations, especially with department heads who felt threatened by his presence and intrusion into their realm.

But with Jean he could be Ry Collier without having to prove anything. He could relax and enjoy himself without having to impress anyone or sell himself as the high-powered executive. Even with the women he dated he never felt he could really be himself. Again, he always seemed to be living up to an image. It was a much needed break from his high profile, fast-paced world. It was an opportunity to sample a different and very appealing aspect of life far removed from his normal routine.

And he liked it.

He picked up his menu. "What captures your fancy?"

"I'm not sure what I have a taste for. Everything looks so good."

Ry ordered a glass of wine for each of them as Jean studied the food selections. And while she was doing that, he studied Jean—the tilt of her head, her glossy hair, the shape of her delicious mouth. Yes, indeed— everything certainly did look good. He reached out and covered her hand with his. He seemed to crave physical contact with her even if it was nothing more than a gentle touching of their hands.

"I think I'm going to have the veal. How about you?"

Jean folded her menu and placed it on the table. "That sounds good to me, too."

The waiter brought their glasses of wine and took their food order. Ry raised his glass toward Jean. "To a lovely lady and many more evenings together."

She felt the heat of her embarrassment flush across her cheeks. "Thank you." Did she dare hope his words were heartfelt and true rather than merely the polite flattery that seemed to come to him so easily?

He reached across the table and placed his hand over hers. "So, what kind of things do you enjoy doing? We can't continue to make going out to dinner our sole entertainment. Do you like concerts? Plays? Museums? Sporting events? Maybe something outdoors such as horseback riding, boating, skiing or hiking? What type of activity is your preference?"

"That's quite a selection of possibilities. I'm not as keen on sporting events, but I like everything you mentioned."

"That gives me a lot to choose from. Do you have any particular favorites?"

"Well, I like music and concerts. I think I've been to every museum in Seattle, some of them numerous times. And I love to do outdoor things. That's one of the things I like so much about living in Seattle. We have both ocean and mountains right here."

A warm sensation of contentment settled inside Jean. Ry seemed to be hanging on every word she said. He made her feel as if what she had to say was important to him. He appeared genuinely interested in what she was saying rather than simply waiting for her to finish so it would be his turn to talk. And he kept the conversation centered around her—what she thought, what she liked—without talking about himself. No one had ever paid that type of undivided attention to her, at least not in a social setting. No one had ever made her feel so very special.

They lingered over an after-dinner drink before leaving the restaurant. They walked hand in hand to his car.

"Thank you for another delightful evening. The movie, dinner—everything was marvelous." She stifled a yawn as she waited for him to unlock the car door.

He cocked his head and allowed a teasing grin to play across his lips. "Bored?"

She quickly recovered. "Not at all. Just a little tired. I need to be at work by seven o'clock tomorrow morning for a meeting with my staff before we start our workday. It's a once a month activity and tomorrow is the day...the first Monday of the month. So...I guess we should call it an evening." The words were well intentioned, but deep down inside she didn't mean them. She wanted to spend more time with Ry, a lot more time—possibly even the entire night. The realization of her thoughts shocked her. She quickly shook away the troublesome notion and all the enticing implications that went with it.

Ry opened the car door for her, then slid in behind the wheel. It seemed as if only a few minutes had passed when he pulled into her driveway. He shut off the engine, then turned to face her as he glanced at his watch. "Are you sure you need to call it a night?" He took hold of her hand. "It's not that late."

A tremor of excitement made its way through her body. She knew she needed to break the physical contact if she was going to maintain her determination to go inside alone while sending Ry home.

"I'm sure. I was up very early this morning and need to be at work very early tomorrow morning." She opened her car door and started to slide out of the seat.

"Well," he said, opening his car door, "the least you can do is let me walk you to your front door and see you safely inside."

As he had done the previous night, he took her key from her hand and unlocked the door for her. He hesitated a moment, hoping she would ask him in. When she took the key from his hand and stepped inside without offering an invitation for coffee, the disappointment flooded through him.

He impulsively grasped her hand, pulled her toward him, then enfolded her in his embrace. A moment later he captured her mouth with a kiss that left nothing to the imagination about what he wanted. His tongue brushed against hers as he sought out the dark recesses of her mouth and reveled in her addictive taste. He twined his fingers in the silky strands of her hair and caressed her shoulders. A moment later a rush of excitement swept through his body as her arms encircled his neck.

He stepped inside the entryway, Jean still wrapped in his arms and the tangible connection of the kiss still intact. He shoved the door shut with his foot. He did not want to leave. He did not want to give up her taste or the way she felt in his arms. He did not want to relinquish the way she drove his senses wild.

Jean's ragged breathing matched his. Her logic and common sense kept pushing at her to put a stop to what was happening before it went any further. Her desires, however, told her it might already be too late. Summoning all her emotional strength, she managed to break the kiss. She took a step back in an attempt to distance herself from thc passion that had nearly overwhelmed her.

"Please…" Her insides shook as she fought to bring her breathing under control. She tried, but was unable to keep the quaver out of her voice. "I think we should call it a night."

He cupped her face in his hands, then reached out a trembling finger and slowly traced the outline of her kiss-swollen lips. The husky quality of his voice said as much as his words. "Are you sure? I'd like very much to stay."

She took another step backward. "Not tonight."

He grasped her hand and started to pull her closer, but she quickly sidestepped his attempt. Her words came out in a breathless rush. "Please, Ry…"

"Okay." He released her hand and gave up a sigh of resignation. "I'll leave, but I certainly don't want to." He placed his hands on her shoulders. "How about dinner tomorrow night?"

"I can't. I have a meeting of my little theater group after work."

"That means I won't see you again until Tuesday evening when we have our dinner with Bill and Susan."

She attempted to force a casual smile which was far removed from the internal battle going on inside her. "Yes, it seems that way."

He drew her to him, placed a tender kiss on her lips, then turned loose of her. "I'll see you Tuesday evening."

Jean watched as he backed out of her driveway and drove away. Would she live to regret the decision she had just made? She tried to approach it in a sensible manner. Spending the night with Ryland Collier was certainly a very appealing idea, but the entire concept was not practical. She could not allow her emotions to carry her away on a cloud of desire. The two of them may have resolved the hurt of the past, but in the present they were little more than strangers. Regardless of their conversation at dinner, their relationship seemed to be built around heated desires and sexual energy rather than really knowing each other as adults.

She took a calming breath. Ry had her emotionally confused. She turned out the lights and went upstairs to her bedroom...alone. She undressed and climbed into bed...alone. She would spend the rest of the night... alone. It was not what she wanted, but she believed it was for the best. Was she only kidding herself?

On Tuesday night, Ry extended a sincere smile across the table toward Bill and Susan. "That was a terrific meal."

Jean quickly agreed with him. "Yes, it was marvelous. Thank you for the treat."

Bill pointedly stared at the way Ry had scooted closer to Jean in the booth and put his arm around her shoulder. He shot a knowing look at Susan before acknowledging the comments. "It was our pleasure. The last couple of weeks have been so hectic. It was nice to be able to kick back and enjoy a quiet meal with good friends."

"And speaking of good friends—" Susan returned Bill's knowing look, then turned her attention to Jean and Ry "—it seems that the two of you are certainly getting along well."

"Of course we are. We've known each other for several years." Ry noted the surprised expressions on Bill's and Susan's faces. "It just took us a little while to figure it out. We went to high school together, lost contact with each other and now have renewed our friendship.''

Susan leaned across the table toward Jean, her excitement evident in her voice. "This is a total surprise. Why didn't you tell me the two of you knew each other?"

Jean cast a sheepish glance toward the table, then out the window before returning to Susan. "I guess I didn't think about it."

"Well, you'll have to tell me all about this."

Bill put his arm around Susan's shoulder and drew her closer to his side. "Don't feel bad, Ry didn't tell me about it, either."

Jean tried to offer what she hoped would be an adequate explanation without going into any of the details. "There really isn't that much to tell. Ry was a year ahead of me in high school. We knew each other for a couple of years before he graduated, then he went away to college and I stayed here."

Ry sensed Jean's reluctance at discussing the topic and moved quickly to relieve her discomfort. He lifted his wineglass toward Bill and Susan to offer a toast. "Here's to a long and happy life for the two of you."

Ry saw the way Susan and Bill looked at each other before taking a drink to seal the toast. It was so obvious how much they loved each other. What must it be like to be so totally head-over-heels in love with someone? And marriage—if there was any such thing as a happy marriage it looked as if Susan and Bill would have it. A wave of despondency washed through him. Maybe it was possible for it to work for some people, but he knew he was not one of them.

He drew Jean closer to him. He had a sudden craving for the closeness and comfort that being with her brought him. Was he getting in over his head? He didn't know, but the possibility left him a little unnerved.

The four of them lingered over coffee and dessert, enjoying casual conversation and an evening of friendship. It felt so real, so comfortable…so settled.

The feeling continued to grow inside Ry as he drove Jean back to her condo. He tried to snap himself out of what he feared was a false sense of well-being. Maybe it felt good now, but it was an intangible that he knew couldn't last. They arrived at her condo. Ry walked her to the door, then went inside without waiting to be invited.

He closed the front door, then pulled her into his embrace. "It was a nice evening, wasn't it? I enjoyed it."

"Yes, Susan and Bill are good company and such a perfect couple. It will be an ideal marriage." Waves of excitement swept through her body as he held her tightly in his arms. It had been only a few days since they had come in contact with each other after fifteen years apart, only a few days since they had resolved the painful past. How could she possibly feel that way about someone in only a few short days?

He placed his fingertips beneath her chin and gently lifted until he could see her eyes. He brushed a soft kiss across her lips, then took a calming breath. He wanted to make love to her, he wanted it more than anything.

"Jean…" He didn't know what to say. It had never been a problem for him before, initiating lovemaking with a desirable woman. But she was different. He captured her mouth with a kiss that quickly deepened in its intensity. His fingers made their way to the front of her blouse and unfastened each button until the garment fell open. He placed a tender kiss on her throat, then scooped her up in his arms.

The cool air hit the bare skin of her chest sending a quick jolt of reality through her passion-clouded senses. What had been escalating euphoria a moment earlier quickly became tinged with a hint of panic. With a great deal of difficulty she broke off the delicious kiss that had worked its way into the very core of her desires. Her words came out as a breathless whisper, almost as much a question as a statement.

"Put me down."

"Jean…"

"Please…" Her eyes searched his, almost pleading. Her fear was not for her physical safety. Far from it. But it was most assuredly fear of the emotional entanglement making love would produce. He hesitated, then lowered her until her feet touched the floor and she stood on her own.

She refastened a couple of the buttons on her blouse, then nervously ran her fingers through her hair smoothing it away from her face. She swallowed in an attempt to tamp down her anxiety. "You…you're rushing me, Ry. I'm not sure I'm ready to take this large a step with you.…" She drew in a steadying breath. "At least not yet. Please give me more time."

He pulled her into his embrace and nestled her head against his shoulder. He drew in several deep breaths and slowly exhaled before speaking. His insides trembled as he attempted to formulate his words. "I'm sorry, Jean. The last thing I want to do is make you feel uncomfortable."

Her words were barely above a whisper. "I know."

He continued to hold her for several minutes, neither of them saying anything. He wasn't sure what he was experiencing at that moment. Certainly disappointment, but something else more intense. He cared about her feelings. He cared very much about her.

He took another calming breath before speaking. "I have a business meeting tomorrow evening and I'm not sure how late it will last. Is it okay if I call you when the meeting is over?"

"Yes, I'd like that."

"And the next night…Thursday…I have access to a couple of very good seats for the jazz concert." He brushed a tender kiss against her lips. "Would you like to go with me?"

A soft smile curled the corners of her lips. "I'd like that, too."

"I'll call you tomorrow night." He gave her a good-night kiss that said far more than his words had.

He reluctantly left her condo and drove back to his hotel. Jean had him completely confused about everything when he used to be so certain. Where he once had shunned the notion of a relationship based on anything more than physical desires, now he found the idea creeping into his thoughts more and more. And those thoughts centered around Jean.

The former Sally Jean Potter, his special high school friend from long ago, now monopolized his thoughts as Jean Summerfield to an extent he never believed could be possible.

And it truly frightened him more than anything ever had.

On Wednesday evening, Ry opened the door to his hotel suite and greeted his visitor. "It's nice to see you again, Matt." He indicated the table where they would conduct their meeting.

Matt Jarvis opened his attaché case and removed a file

folder. "It's like I explained to you, Ry, a furniture man-ufacturing company has some special problems not pres-ent in other manufacturing situations, especially ours where we do custom work and very little assembly-line-type of production. I know we are in serious need of instituting some new streamlined methods, but I don't know where or how to begin. I'm particularly concerned about the personnel department. It seems to be a quag-mire of unrelated things and I'm not sure how to straighten it out. My personnel manager does a marvel-ous job with what has been handed her, but there has to be some easier way to handle all the bits and pieces of stuff that gets thrown her way."

Matt leveled his steady gaze at Ry. "So, how do you want to proceed on Monday morning?"

"It will probably be easier if you and I go from de-partment to department where you can introduce me and explain why I'm there. It will be less disruptive than shutting down everything and calling all the employees together in one place. I'd like to spend the first week just observing the various departments and watching how they interrelate, then I'll spend concentrated time in each department to study their flow system. At the end of the four weeks I'll present you with a written report of my findings along with detailed recommendations for im-proved efficiency within each department and a better flow between departments and an overall restructuring plan for the company."

"That sounds good to me." Matt opened a file folder. "Here are some of my concerns and areas where I'd like you to pay particular attention." He handed several sheets of paper to Ry.

The meeting continued for another three hours with Ry and Matt discussing the areas of concern and the

procedures Ry would be using for his four week evaluation. Finally Matt closed his attaché case and left Ry's
hotel suite. Ry made some additional notes and added
them to his file, then set the work project aside. His mind
was filled with so many thoughts of Jean that any more
work had become nearly impossible. Even if he couldn't
see her that night he could at least talk to her and hear
her voice.

He dialed her number. "Hi, I didn't wake you, did I?
I'm sorry to be calling so late."

"No, you didn't wake me. I was watching the news."

"I would have called earlier, but my client just left.
The meeting went a little longer than I had anticipated.
I had hoped it would end early enough for us to still be
able to do something tonight." He hesitated, not sure of
exactly how to express himself. "I'm still willing. How
about you? I could be at your place in a few minutes."

A soft laugh traveled the phone line to his ear. "Not
tonight. I'm already in my pajamas and will be headed
for bed as soon as the news is over."

He started to make a comment about helping her to
her bedroom, but held his words. Even though he knew
she would tell him it was too late for them to see each
other that night, it did not stop the twinge of disappointment from assailing his senses. "Yes, you're right. It is
too late. Are we still on for the jazz concert tomorrow
night? I'll pick you up at seven o'clock. Will that be
okay?"

"That will be perfect. I'll see you then. Good night."

"Good night." Ry hung up the phone, but allowed his
hand to linger on the receiver after placing it in the cra-
dle. He wanted to share everything with her, be part of
everything she did. It was a very new feeling for him,
something he had not experienced before. But exactly

what did it mean? He didn't really know if he wanted an answer to that question.

Following the concert Thursday night, they returned to Jean's condo. Ry unlocked Jean's front door, then handed the key to her. "Great concert. I can still feel the electricity in the air," he said.

"I totally agree. What an exciting performance. The music is still coursing inside me." Her words may have been enthusiastic, but her concerns for what the evening's culmination would bring had been growing inside her on the drive back to her condo. She stepped inside, hesitated, then moved aside so he could enter the living room.

It was a moment that had been preying on her mind for the past half hour, ever since the end of the jazz concert. Would she be able to continue resisting his all-too-tempting manner? Or perhaps a better question might be to ask herself if she would be able to resist her own heated desires where Ry Collier was concerned.

"Would you like some coffee?"

"That would be nice, thank you."

She went to the kitchen with Ry following right behind her. As soon as she stopped walking, he pulled her into his embrace.

She started to take a step backward as she emitted a bit of a self-conscious chuckle. "Ry, I haven't had a chance to make the coffee yet."

"That's okay. I don't really want any coffee." He quickly captured her mouth with a kiss that went from casual to passionate in less than a second. He ran his hand down her back, across her hip and finally cupped her bottom. He pulled her hips closer, snuggling them against his.

The moment of her concern had arrived. She felt his growing hardness press against her. Then, as if her arms had a will and mind of their own, they circled around his neck and she returned his kiss with an amount of fervor equal to his. She felt herself being drawn further and further into the magnetic web of his masculinity. And with each passing second she grew less and less certain about her ability to maintain any control over what was happening. Her thoughts swirled around in a fog. One second she wanted to make love with Ry and then the next she knew she had to break it off before it was too late.

With a great deal of difficulty she managed to end the delicious kiss that had consumed her much like an out of control wildfire. She fought to bring her ragged breathing under control before attempting to speak.

"Please, Ry…you're rushing me."

He attempted to force his labored breathing into a calmer mode without much success. "I don't mean to." He took another steadying breath as he cradled her head against his shoulder. "You are so desirable…and so very special. It's just that I—" He bit off his words before he said any more. He had already said too much.

"I'm sorry, Jean. I'd better go." Even though it was his stated intention, it was the last thing he wanted to do. He refused to release her from his embrace, continuing to hold her body tightly against his as he stroked her hair and reveled in the sensation of warmth and contentment he experienced from just being with her.

"Perhaps that would be best." Her emotions were torn in several directions. The last thing she really wanted was for him to leave, but her fear of what might happen if she allowed herself to give in to her desires won out. She already knew she was emotionally involved far more than she wanted to be. She was so confused about what to do—follow her desires or do what she knew would be the logical and responsible thing.

An unpleasant thought struck her, one she found very upsetting. A sinking feeling settled in the pit of her stomach. What about Ry? Did he think she was playing teasing games with him? She had to say something to let him know it wasn't so. She looked up into the depths of his silver eyes—eyes that had clouded to a sensual smoky-gray.

Ry brushed his fingertips tenderly across her cheek. He saw the question in her eyes, but didn't know what it was or why it was there. "Jean? Is there something bothering you? Are you upset with me? I hope not."

She swallowed her nervousness and tried to sound confident. "No, I'm not upset with you. I was just concerned about you thinking I was...uh..." Embarrassment forced her to glance down at the floor, unable to hold the eye contact any longer. "Well, I was afraid you might think I was just leading you on...teasing you. That I was—"

He placed his fingertips against her lips to still her words. "No, that thought never crossed my mind and you should erase it from yours. I know you're not that kind of woman."

He continued to hold her as the moments passed, neither of them saying anything. It was a strange mixture of contentment and anxiety. He didn't know where any of this was headed, but he knew it could not continue as it was. He could not allow her to slip away from his life again, but what was he willing to offer her to keep her from going? He didn't know what to do or what to say about the future, about whether they even had a future together.

A few minutes later Ry reluctantly departed. He had been so torn about what to do. As much as he wanted to stay, even if they didn't make love, he sensed how uneasy she was with the spot he had put her in. He had no business pushing her like that. She was not the type of woman who would engage in a short-term sexual affair with no strings attached. No matter how much he wanted her, he had to keep that fact in mind. He didn't want a shallow relationship with her, something based on nothing more than how physically excited they were. He wanted something much deeper, much more important. But exactly how much more was still a mystery to him, a concept that had him confused.

He returned to his hotel suite and fell into an uneasy sleep. Images of Jean danced through his dreams, leaving him torn between his fears of commitment to a relationship and what life could be like with her.

Ry picked Jean up early Saturday morning and they took the ferry from Seattle to Bainbridge Island. They drove across the bridge at the back of the island to the Olympic Peninsula, around to Port Angeles and then to Olympic National Park for a picnic. It was a perfect autumn day with blue skies and bright sunshine.

They spread a blanket on the ground, then unpacked the picnic basket. They enjoyed a lunch of fried chicken, potato salad and fresh fruit. Following lunch Ry sat on the blanket, his back against a large rock. He snuggled Jean in between his outstretched legs with her back resting against his chest. He drew in a deep breath, held it for a moment, then exhaled with a sigh of contentment.

He draped his arms over her shoulders, inching up the bottom of her pullover shirt until he had it hiked up above her breasts. Everything about being with Jean felt so right, so comfortable, so perfect. She was very important to his life. He tickled his fingers along the edge of her lacy bra, surprised to find that it hooked in front. A moment later he had unfastened the hooks exposing her bare breasts to his hands.

The sensation of her bare skin, of her tautly puckered nipples pushing into the palm of his hands, sent a tingle of excitement through his body. He wanted to make love to her at that moment and at that spot with the fresh air and sunshine surrounding them, the sounds of birds and the leaves rustling in the breeze. The day was, indeed, perfect. But he was ever mindful of her words about rushing her. He wasn't sure what to do, how to proceed.

"That was a great lunch you packed. I'm afraid I made a real pig of myself." He bent forward and placed a tender kiss on the side of her neck, then rested his cheek against the top of her head. "Did I leave you enough to eat?" He reveled in the delight of her bare breasts nestled in his hands.

She responded to his words with a soft laugh and to his sensual touch with a tremor of delight. "Yes, you left plenty of food for me."

She glanced up toward the treetops. The sunlight filtered through the leaves creating mottled patterns of light and shadow on the ground. The happiness she felt at that moment settled over her like a gossamer veil, her senses acutely aware of his touch and wanting more.

"This is idyllic. It would be marvelous if we could spend the rest of the day here." She could not stop the thought telling her how exciting it would be for them to make love right there at that moment. But, of course, they couldn't if for no other reason than they didn't have the time. That evening was the rehearsal and the rehearsal dinner and they both needed to attend.

"Yes, it would…" He slid one of his hands down her stomach toward the top of her jeans, then hesitated for a moment. He ended up wrapping his arm around her waist. He scooted away from the rock until he was able to stretch out on the blanket. He pulled Jean down on top of him, then turned over until his body partially covered hers.

He captured her mouth with a demanding kiss, but not more demanding than she was willing to return. Tremors of excitement coursed through her veins. Her body tingled with anticipation. Her ragged breathing shoved her bare breasts against his chest. His hand slid across the bare skin of her back, coming to rest just inside the top of her jeans.

With a great deal of reluctance, Jean reached behind and placed her hand on top of his to stop him from moving his hand any lower. She broke off the delicious kiss and fought to bring her breathing under control. "Ry, this isn't the right time or place."

His breathing was as labored as hers as he rose up on one elbow. "It feels right to me." He lowered his head and teased her nipple with the tip of his tongue, then drew it into his mouth.

A quick gasp followed by a wave of sensual delight told Jean just how much she wanted Ry to make love to her. But she knew things had already gone much further than she should have allowed. She finally managed a bit of control of her desires. "We…we need to start back to Seattle so we can get ready for tonight."

Ry allowed the delicious treat to slip from his mouth. He placed a tender kiss on her breast, then reluctantly sat up. "Yes, you're right." The disappointment burrowed into his consciousness, but was tempered by the knowledge that he knew she had made the logical decision for the circumstances.

Jean sat upright. She experienced an immediate sense of loss when he withdrew the warmth of his touch. She quickly hooked her bra and lowered the hem of her shirt.

Ry pulled her into his arms and placed a tender kiss on her lips. "Thank you for spending the day with me."

She wrapped her arms around his waist. "I had a marvelous time today. A picnic was a great idea. I only wish we didn't have to rush back to town—"

The full impact of the words hit her. "Oh, I didn't mean that the way it sounded. I certainly didn't mean to imply that I didn't want to go to the rehearsal—"

Ry placed his fingertips against her lips as a soft chuckle escaped his throat. "I know what you mean and I agree. I wish we didn't have to rush back right away, either."

He lowered his head and captured her mouth with a kiss that once again sent tremors of delight through her body—a toe curling kiss that left her weak in the knees. Every time he kissed her she felt herself being drawn further and further into an emotional whirlwind that centered around Ry Collier. She could still feel the heat of his touch on her skin, his hands cupping her bare breasts, his mouth on her nipple. Was it infatuation or physical desire? Or was she actually falling in love with him? She didn't know, but the possibilities frightened her.

Jean reluctantly broke off the kiss. "I think we'd better get going. If we run into too much traffic at the ferry dock, we could be delayed waiting for the next ferry to Seattle."

He brushed another quick kiss across her lips. "You're right. It wouldn't do to be late for the rehearsal."

"Since we're running so short on time I think you should drop me off at my place and go on ahead. I'll shower, change clothes and meet you at the rehearsal."

She returned the items to the picnic basket while Ry shook out the blanket and folded it. He took the basket from her and put everything in the trunk of his car. They got in the car and he started the drive back to town.

Ry reached over and took her hand while driving. He may have said the words, but it was a far cry from what he felt and what he wanted. Even though Bill Todd was his best friend and it was a privilege to serve as Bill's best man, he wanted to spend all his time with Jean…just the two of them. He had wanted to make love to her under the trees with the sun shining on their bare skin.

An odd emptiness combined with the emotional tug that invaded his reality whenever they were apart. He could still feel the sensation of her silky skin, of her breasts in the palms of his hands and the taste of her puckered nipple. A little shudder of apprehension made its way through his body. The emotional part of that equation left him uneasy. He didn't need or want a relationship. The word relationship smacked of commitment and it was the one thing that truly terrified him more than anything else. He glanced over at Jean. Her head rested against the back of the seat and her eyes were closed. He gave her hand a little squeeze.

"Are you asleep?"

She opened her eyes and offered him a smile. Her words were soft, almost introspective. "No. I was just thinking about everything that's happened this past week, of the strange turn of events that brought us here today. Just a week and a day ago I wouldn't have believed a painful experience from fifteen years ago could turn out like this."

They arrived at the dock on Bainbridge Island and were able to board the next ferry for downtown Seattle. As soon as their car was parked on the vehicle level, they went upstairs and out on the deck. They stood next to the railing, his arm around her shoulder, watching the Seattle skyline growing closer. It had been several minutes since any words had been spoken. Words seemed unnecessary.

It was finally Ry who broke the silence. His voice was soft, his words heartfelt as he pulled her into his arms. "Thank you for spending a perfect day with me."

The breeze ruffled through her hair, the cool air from the ocean reminding her that the delights of the Indian summer would soon be gone and winter would be approaching. She snuggled into his embrace, reveling in the warmth and closeness. "It was my pleasure. I enjoyed it very much."

He caressed her back and held her closer. "Are you cold? Do you want me to get your sweater from the car?"

"No, I'm fine." As long as she was in his arms nothing could be wrong. Again the silence pervaded. Only the sounds of the seagulls and the ferry boat moving through the water broke the silence. A feeling of peace settled over her, filling her with the type of contentment she had never before known.

And a second later his mouth was on hers.

Ry's passion infused her with a heated desire that sent a tingling excitement coursing through her body, very similar to the sensation she experienced when he took her nipple into his mouth. Certainly physical desire. But mere infatuation? No matter how much she denied it, things had moved far beyond infatuation. In her heart she truly suspected she might be falling in love with him regardless of how much she didn't want it to be true. Once again she was losing her heart to someone in spite of her intentions to never do it again. One bad marriage plus a very painful affair had been more than enough involvement for one lifetime. Then all her thoughts stopped and she gave herself over to the exhilaration building inside her.

Ry tightened his hold on her as the kiss deepened. The hum and thump of the ferry engines reverberated through his body, feeding into the sensual desires coursing through his veins. She was everything he wanted. She was exactly what he wanted. But commitment to a relationship? Just the thought sent a jolt of panic through his consciousness. He broke off the kiss and cradled her head against his shoulder. For a brief moment he wished they could stay in that spot just as they were, forever in each other's arms.

The announcement over the loudspeaker intruded into their reverie. Car passengers were instructed to return to their vehicles in preparation for arrival at the ferry dock in downtown Seattle. The tender moment between them had been broken.

One thing kept circulating through the back of Jean's mind. What would happen following the rehearsal dinner? She had managed to curb her desires so far and hold off Ry, but how much longer could she keep that up? That afternoon had been the most severe test of her resolve. Ry had been very gracious in the way he had deferred to her wishes. The uncertainty of the situation finally disappeared as the conscious thought crystallized in her mind. She had made her decision. Tonight, following the rehearsal dinner....

She allowed a little frown to wrinkle across her brow. The decision to make love with him would take them down an unknown path, one that could lead to love or disaster. An uneasiness tried to replace the positive feeling. She shoved it aside. If she was falling for Ry Collier—

If…that was a laugh. She knew in her heart that it had gone beyond the *if* stage. She was far too involved to turn back now. But would it be something she would live to regret?

Four

Everyone was in a festive mood as Jean and Ry entered the banquet room at the hotel following the rehearsal at the church. When all the participants had been seated and champagne poured, Ry stood and offered a toast to the bride and groom. Excitement ran high and the champagne continued to flow into the night even after all the dinner dishes had been cleared away.

Tomorrow was the big day, the culmination of all the many preparations. The next afternoon, following the wedding reception, Susan and Bill would be off to Paris for their honeymoon. It had been a week filled with fun as well as the emotional togetherness of close friends. Susan had wanted a large traditional wedding and Jean had helped her plan it. She had been so happy for her friend. The depth of Susan's and Bill's love was so obvious. She could see it every time they looked at each other.

A moment of sadness swept over Jean. Would she ever know that kind of love? To love and be loved in return with such devotion? She shook away the negative thought. This was a time for happiness, not intrusive doubts.

Ry leaned over to Jean, took her hand in his and whispered in her ear. "Half the guests have already gone. I think it would be all right if we said our goodbyes and left. Why don't we sneak away and go someplace else where we can have a quiet drink...just the two of us?"

Her voice was hesitant as her common sense did battle with her desires and her euphoric mood. "I don't know." In spite of her earlier decision to make love with him, now that the moment was at hand the panic welled inside her, producing doubts. "It's late and we've both consumed a lot of champagne, at least I know I've had more than my share. I've already decided to take a cab home and leave my car here in the parking garage." It was the truth, as far as it went. But an even greater truth was the way her desires tore down her resistance and eroded her resolve.

His breath tickled across her cheek sending little shivers of delight across her skin, then his lips nibbled at her earlobe. "You're right. So let's stay here. We can go up to my suite and have a quiet drink before calling it an evening. I'll personally put you in a cab for a safe trip home as soon as you want to leave."

The shivers of delight turned to tremors of excitement. It had been a fantastic week filled with more fun and happiness than she had ever known. It had also been filled with an intense sexual chemistry that she could not deny even if she wanted to. She succumbed to the desires coursing through her veins, desires that were as much emotional as they were physical.

She returned his smile. "I'd like that."

After thanking their host and hostess, they slipped quietly out of the banquet room and walked hand in hand toward the elevator. A few minutes later Jean kicked off her shoes and Ry took off his suit coat, loosened his tie and unfastened the top button of his shirt. He turned on the stereo, then pulled her into his arms and held her as they swayed to the soft music without actually dancing.

She was everything any man could want and he definitely wanted her. He wasn't sure exactly what had been happening between them, but it left him both apprehensive and enthralled. She felt good in his arms and he knew she would feel even better in his bed. He caressed her shoulders as he pulled her body closer to his. A rush of lustful desire swirled around inside him becoming entwined with emotions he didn't want to acknowledge. His breathing quickened.

He kissed the side of her neck, then slid his mouth across to hers. His heart pounded in his chest. With slightly trembling fingers he slowly lowered the zipper down the back of her dress.

Jean had anticipated the moment with an almost out of control excitement. She quickly shoved away the fears and apprehensions that tried to pull at her. There was no doubt in her mind that making love with Ryland Collier would be something very special—at the very least a memory to live inside her for the rest of her life.

His hand tickled across the bare skin of her back sending tremors of delight through her body. The fears that continued to dwell in her consciousness were not strong enough to overcome the desires and emotions welling inside her. She undid his tie and pulled it from around his neck. Then she reached for the buttons on his shirt and began to unfasten them.

He captured her mouth with an intense kiss that promised a world of passion. Her breathing turned ragged as she melted into the aura of sensuality emanating from him. She managed to undo two of his shirt buttons before her trembling fingers refused to cooperate. The music from the stereo disappeared from her mind to be replaced by the sound of her pounding heart and her labored breathing.

A shiver of sweet anticipation flitted across the surface of her skin as Ry eased her dress from her shoulders. It dropped down past her hips, fell to the floor and pooled at her feet. The cool air wafted across her bare skin. He scooped her up in his arms and she snuggled into the warmth as he carried her through the door to the bedroom. He gently placed her in the middle of the king-size bed.

There would be no turning back, Ry realized. He wasn't sure he could stop even if he wanted to. The taste of Jean's mouth, the creamy texture of her skin, the silkiness of her hair—everything about her sent his desires soaring. He tore at the buttons on his shirt in a frantic effort to rid himself of the garment, finally dropping the shirt on the floor. An odd sensation pushed its way through his body as he gazed at her beautiful face and the way her chestnut hair spread across the pillow. She wore only panty hose with lace bikini panties under them. Her bare breasts tempted his touch the same way they had that afternoon, but his control of the situation had disintegrated.

The emotional impact of what was about to happen tried to gain a foothold, but he shoved the emotions aside. He reached out a trembling hand and gently stroked her cheek. He trailed his fingertips down the side of her neck, across her shoulder and finally cupped her breast in his hand. Her eyes glowed with a sensual enticement that no man in his right mind could possibly resist.

His words were a husky whisper, his voice thick with the emotion he had tried so hard to deny. "Sally Jean, you are absolutely exquisite." Her tautly puckered nipple pushed into his hand as she arched her back. He quickly moved to draw the delicious treat into his mouth. The overwhelming intensity of the moment sent a quick shock wave through his body.

A rush of heated passion surged through Jean the moment his mouth came in contact with her breast. She gasped for air as she jerked her head back into the softness of the pillow. She ran her hands across the hard muscled planes of his chest, the sensation sending a tingling excitement to her already stimulated senses. Her mind whirled in a fog, her only clear thought the sensual delights they were about to share.

His hardened arousal pressed against her thigh. She reached for the waist of his slacks and fumbled with his belt buckle in an attempt to undo it. When that failed, she tugged at the tops of her panty hose. She desperately wanted to be free of the last remnants of her clothes, to revel in the feel of his bare skin along the length of her body.

Ry allowed her nipple to slip from his mouth, the wet bud glistening in the soft light. Slow…he wanted to take things slow and savor every delicious moment. But his frenetic motions belied his intentions as he quickly disposed of the rest of his clothes. He tossed his slacks and briefs on the floor. As soon as he was free of the encumbrances of his clothes he turned his gaze on her.

She was a beautiful sight—the silken strands of her chestnut hair in disarray, her cheeks and forehead flushed with excitement, her eyes glistening with desire. Slow might have been his intention, but the reality wasn't as easily accomplished. He kissed her throat as he cupped her breasts in his hands. He teased each puckered nipple with his mouth, then trailed the tip of his tongue down between her breasts. His labored breathing pounded in his chest. His pulse raced.

He slipped his hands underneath her body, working them inside the back of her panty hose and panties until he could cup the perfect roundness of her bare bottom. He nipped at the waistband with his teeth and slowly worked her panty hose and panties down her hips, finally finishing the job with his hands by pulling them completely off and dropping them on the floor.

He quickly stretched out next to her, the length of his body partly covering hers. His mouth came down on hers with a forceful passion that demanded as much as it gave. His hand slid effortlessly down her rib cage and across her hip, her skin smooth and creamy to his touch.

A heated tremor of delight followed in the wake of his caress. Her blood rushed hot through her veins. Her pulse throbbed in a matching cadence with her pounding heart. Every sensor in her body felt more alive than ever before. She reached for his hardness, her fingers wrapping around the girth of his rigidity. A moment later the sensation of his fingers tickling up the inside of her thigh sent an incendiary wave crashing through her.

Then his hand was at the core of her femininity. She felt the gasp leave her throat as much as she heard it. His tongue twined with hers, their mouths eagerly matching the way his fingers penetrated the moist heat of her sex and her fingers stroked his manhood. She arched her hips, wanting more of his attentions. Then the delicious convulsions started, quickly spreading through her body and setting every nerve ending on fire.

He settled his body between her legs sending an incredibly intense jolt of desire sweeping through her body. Images, thoughts, feelings…everything swirled around in her head enhanced by the champagne and an evening immersed in an atmosphere of love, marriage and honeymoons. Somewhere in the back of her mind a warning bell tried to grab her attention, but she ignored it. She didn't want anything to interfere with the delicious sensations racing through her body and the promise of what was to be. All she wanted was Ry Collier.

As much as he wanted to prolong the foreplay, Ry could not postpone his overwhelming desire for that final intimate connection, the physical union of their bodies into one. He had never wanted anyone as much in his entire life. The heat of her excitement radiated to the core of his life.

He broke the kiss, but only for a moment—only long enough to gasp, "Sally Jean…" then his mouth was on hers again. He tried to form some sort of conscious thought, but his raging desires shoved everything else out of the way.

He slowly penetrated the core of her womanhood with his hardened arousal, the sensation so intense that it nearly took his breath away. He tried to set a slow pace, to establish a smooth rhythm. Each of his thrusts were met by an enthusiastic response from her as they moved together as if they were long-time lovers. Time seemed to stand still as he reveled in the intense feelings coursing through his body. They were one and it was exquisite.

Her arms tightened around him. Her gasp of euphoria spurred his release of ecstasy. His body stiffened. He tightened his hold on her as hard spasms shot down through his thighs and up to his chest. It was the most breathtaking sensation—the most profound lovemaking of his life. His pulse raced in wild abandon, but his mind was a blank. He couldn't get any thoughts to crystallize other than the one that told him being with Jean was what made it so special.

His breathing slowly returned to normal. He stroked her hair, brushing the loose tendrils away from her damp cheek. The dim light glistened on the thin sheen of perspiration that covered her face. The fire of passion glowed in her eyes as it reached out to him. He felt himself being drawn into an emotional whirlwind that left him ecstatic and frightened all at the same time. He caressed her shoulders, not wanting to release her from his embrace.

Jean finally managed to bring her ragged breathing under control. She had never felt so totally satisfied in her entire life. Everything she had ever dreamed about Ry Collier had come true. He was without a doubt the most exciting and giving lover any woman could ever wish for. Their lovemaking had been the most significant and exciting event of her life.

She allowed a soft moan of desire when Ry cupped her breast, gently manipulating her hardened nipple between his fingers. His lips nibbled at her earlobe, then a moment later they were on her mouth with a sizzling determination. The fiery passion of their coupling hadn't even died down when the flames burst into a renewed fervor of unbridled lovemaking.

Ry opened one eye just enough to see that the digital clock on the nightstand read nine o'clock. The bright morning sun filtered in through the drapes. It was much later than he thought it would be. Normally he would have been out of bed a couple of hours ago if not earlier, but it was very late last night when they had finally fallen asleep. A warm sensation enveloped him as he thought about the reason why it had been so late. Even though he was now fully awake, he closed his eyes and allowed his mind to drift over everything that had happened.

It had been an incredible night, so much more than he ever imagined or anticipated. Jean was in his bed, wrapped in his embrace and sleeping next to him. It was a sensation he didn't want to ever lose. A dark cloud invaded his glow of contentment. What type of personal price would he have to pay to keep it? He knew the cost would be high. At the very least it would require a commitment to a relationship. Was that too high a price? Higher than he could afford to pay? Or was willing to pay?

Had he purposely seduced her with champagne to break down her resolve? Were his intentions less than honorable? Had he taken advantage of her in spite of the fact that she had previously told him he was rushing her? And now that they had made love, what would she be expecting from him?

They had made love with an intensity greater than any he had ever known and it had made a major impact on his reality. He knew he was far more emotionally involved than he had intended, than he had ever been before and much more than he had wanted to be.

And that truly frightened him beyond anything he had ever encountered or imagined.

He tried to shove the disturbing thought from his mind and dwell instead on the warm glow of contentment their lovemaking had produced. But his attempts were short-lived as the disturbing thoughts returned. The magnitude of his emotions were something he didn't want to deal with. There was no way a true relationship would ever work. The only commitment he was interested in was to his work and building his fortune. Maybe he would have room to handle a commitment after he met his goal of twenty million dollars by his thirty-fifth birthday. Jean stirred, drawing his attention away from his troublesome thoughts.

The veil of sleep lifted from Jean's brain as she rolled over on to her side. A soft warmth spread through her as Ry slid his hand across her stomach so that his arm encircled her body. She had never experienced anything as overwhelming as the lovemaking they had shared. Before last night she thought she might be falling in love with him. But in the wake of their lovemaking and with the new day she realized there was no longer any doubt or uncertainty. She was in love with Ry Collier. What she didn't know was what to do about it.

Their lovemaking had been surrounded by an almost frenzied sense of urgency. They couldn't keep their hands off each other. It had been like an out of control wildfire that couldn't be stopped. All the pent-up sexual tension had escaped in an incendiary explosion. There had been no thought to what the morning would bring, only the immediacy of the here and now. She had been swept up into a whirlwind of desire and fulfillment and the euphoric afterglow continued to radiate inside her.

Then stark reality knocked the dreamy contentment from her mind, replacing it with a cold jolt of anxiety. A warning thought had tried to get through her clouded mind before they made love, but she had refused to accept it. What had been euphoria just moments earlier had quickly turned to alarm. They had been so single-minded about their lovemaking that they had failed to take precautions. A cold shudder attacked her senses. Ry had not used a condom.

She took a calming breath in an attempt to still her rapidly growing trepidation. *It will be okay. The chances of me getting pregnant are remote. There's nothing to worry about.* The words played over and over in her mind. She wanted to believe them. She tried to believe them. She needed to believe them. But that didn't stop her anxiety from turning to panic.

Pregnant...what if she ended up pregnant? What would she do? What would she say to Ry? What would Ry think?

"Are you awake?" Ry asked.

His words interrupted her escalating fears, bringing them to a momentary halt. She managed a soft whisper. "Yes, I'm awake."

"Are you okay? You don't have any regrets about last night?"

His words tickled across her senses bringing back the warm glow she had experienced upon waking. "Regrets? No, I don't have any regrets." Regrets that they had made love? Regrets that she had experienced the most incredible night of her life? Absolutely not.

Then the dark cloud of doubt presented itself again. But, regrets about their lapse of good sense in not using a condom? A little shiver darted through her body. She hoped she would not have cause for regrets.

He kissed her cheek before reluctantly working his arm out from under her and relinquishing his embrace. An immediate sense of loss told him more than he wanted to know about his emotional involvement. He tried to keep his voice neutral so that none of the deep emotion coursing through him would escape into the open to betray his inner feelings. "It's late. It's after nine o'clock."

Shock hit her and surprise surrounded her words. "Nine o'clock? I had no idea it was that late."

"And we have a wedding to attend that starts at two o'clock."

She sat up, taking the sheet with her to cover her nude body. Her fully alert mind caught the distance that had crept into his voice. It sent a wave of trepidation through her. Was it her imagination or was it his way of telling her that this was all there would ever be? That any type of an ongoing relationship was out of the question? That they didn't have a future together, at least not the type of future she would want? Had she again lost her heart to someone who would use it badly then leave?

She forced a blasé outer manner to match his, desperate to keep her true emotions hidden. She was not that schoolgirl of fifteen years ago and she knew that fantasies had no place in real life. She had eagerly walked into last night with her eyes wide-open to what she was doing in spite of all the champagne and the sensual atmosphere. It had definitely been the most glorious night of her life. Accepting responsibility for her own actions was not a problem.

She would show Ry that she could be as casual about things as he was, that she was certainly not putting any pressure on him. "You're right. I need to go home. I must look a mess. I'll have to hurry if I'm going to be at the church in time to help Susan get ready." She glanced around the bedroom while shoving down her mounting trepidation. "Now, if I could just remember where I left my clothes."

Ry climbed out of bed and moved quickly toward the closet. "Let me get one of the hotel robes for you." He felt the chill in the air and knew it wasn't due to the temperature. What had been heated passion last night had turned to cool civility. What should have been an intimate time of touching, stroking and murmured tenderness had turned into awkward politeness. Circumstances could be blamed for part of it, the time constraint that said they needed to hurry to get ready for the wedding. But he knew he was as much to blame.

He handed the robe to her and then put on the other one. "I'll make some coffee."

"No..." She pulled on the robe, then slid out of bed. "I really don't have time. I need to go home. I promised Susan I'd be at the church by noon to help her with her hair and clothes. That doesn't leave very much time for me to get ready."

"I...uh...I suppose you're right." The nervous tension churned in the pit of his stomach. He knew he needed to say something to her to reassure her about last night. Something to tell her that he had not taken their lovemaking lightly. Quite the contrary. It had been more profound than anything he had ever experienced, but the emotions attached to it were more than he could handle.

He watched as she collected her clothes, then disappeared into the bathroom. He needed to clear out his thoughts, to get some sort of logical handle on what was happening. He wandered into the parlor room of the suite. He made coffee and as soon as it was ready poured himself a cup. If only the wedding wasn't in a few hours. If only he had some time in which to try to figure everything out.

He heard the bathroom door open and a moment later Jean stood in the doorway between the bedroom and the parlor. She was dressed and obviously ready to leave.

"If you wait a couple of minutes I'll throw on some clothes and walk you to your car."

"No, there's no need."

"Are you sure? It will only take a couple of minutes for me to get dressed."

"I'll see you at the church." She turned toward the front door.

"Jean...." He didn't know what to say. He stood there feeling totally helpless. Even though they would be seeing each other in a few hours, he couldn't let her walk out, not like this. A cold shiver of anxiety darted through his body. Exactly where did things stand between them? Was he about to make as big a blunder as he had fifteen years ago? She was the type who would want a commitment. She was also the type who deserved one. But it was the one thing he couldn't offer her.

In spite of that, he couldn't let her just walk out the door without saying or doing something. He pulled her into his arms and held her tightly for a moment, desperately wanting to cling to the sensual warmth they had shared in his bed. Her arms slipped around his waist. He cradled her head against his shoulder and stroked her hair. "Are you sure you're all right?"

"Yes, I'm fine. I'm just feeling a little stressed because of the late hour. I have lots to do."

"Jean...." He took a steadying breath, then spoke words that were far removed from what he wished he could have said to her. "I'll see you at the church."

Something about his tone of voice and the expression on her face made her insides quiver. He had started to say something, but had obviously changed his mind. He hadn't been rude or cold, but there was definitely a distance.

She left his suite and walked quickly down the hall to

the elevator. A few minutes later she was in her car on the way home. She had to dismiss the troublesome thoughts from her mind and concentrate on the wedding. Susan would need her help, but she had to get herself together first.

As soon as she arrived home she took a shower, washed her hair and set it with her hot rollers. She laid out her clothes and expertly applied her makeup while keeping a close watch on the clock. But as busy as she was, her thoughts were filled with Ry Collier and not the wedding of her best friend.

Jean finished getting ready, then hurried to the church, arriving at the same time as Susan. The two women immediately went to work. Susan's nervousness and Jean's desire to calm her friend temporarily took her mind off her concerns about Ry and where they were headed, but it could not totally erase her lurking fear about the possibility of their lapse in judgment resulting in her being pregnant.

The hour of the wedding finally arrived. She had not seen Ry yet, but that was understandable. As best man he was with Bill. The groom, best man and groomsmen would enter from a side door, with the bride, maid of honor and bridesmaids entering from the back and walking up the center aisle.

Jean beamed at her friend as she handed Susan the bridal bouquet. "You look beautiful. Without a doubt the most stunning bride to ever walk down the aisle."

Susan gave Jean a quick hug. "Right now I feel like my legs are going to buckle under me. This is ridiculous. I'm too old to be this kind of nervous. This is for someone who's only twenty-one or twenty-two, not a mature woman of twenty-nine, who will be thirty years old in a couple of months."

"Nonsense. Everything will go perfectly." Jean turned her head toward the door. "There's the music. It's time." She straightened a twist in Susan's veil, gave her friend a quick wink, then got in line for her entrance into the sanctuary.

As Jean walked down the aisle, her first glimpse of Ry in his tux literally took her breath away. He looked so incredibly handsome and elegant. He was everything she had ever wanted, everything she had been searching for all her life. She had endured a miserable marriage with a man who not only cheated on her at every turn, but who treated her as if she was his property.

She had met Jerry Summerfield during her junior year of college. The overweight, insecure Sally Jean had immediately fallen under his spell as he flattered her with empty words. She had thought she was in love with him when she accepted his marriage proposal, but less than three months later she started to suspect he was cheating on her. He had become indifferent to her and her needs and treated her more like a housekeeper than a wife. She finally came to the realization that the marriage was over even though they had been married only two years. The breaking moment had come when she returned home from work early one afternoon to find him in bed with another woman. She had filed for divorce the next day.

And then she had survived the betrayal of a disastrous relationship following her marriage, a relationship she had thought would last forever. At that time she had sworn she would never give her heart away again. She had made her own life and become her own person, but there was still an emptiness inside her…a desire for a family of her own.

She mechanically went through the motions of the ceremony without giving it any conscious thought. Her mind was filled with so many other things and all of them centered around Ryland Collier. When Ry took her arm for them to walk up the aisle behind the newly married bride and groom, it startled her out of her thoughts. She had been so consumed by her own concerns that she hadn't realized the ceremony was over.

Ry's whispered words tickled across her cheek as he gave her hand a quick squeeze. "Funny the way things change now that it's all legal. Susan looks relieved, but now Bill looks nervous." A soft chuckle surrounded his words. "He's probably just realizing what he's gotten himself into."

She whispered her response. "Is that the confirmed bachelor talking?" She wasn't sure if she was joking with him or asking a serious question. She didn't pursue the conversation. Either way, it was not the time or the place.

The wedding party and invited guests moved to the hotel banquet room for the reception. Everyone was in a very festive mood. There was the traditional cutting of the wedding cake and plenty of champagne.

Ry handed a glass to Jean. She hesitated a moment, then took the offered champagne. "I don't know if I should. I had enough of this yesterday evening to last me for quite a while."

His brow furrowed for a moment. His words were part concern for her feelings and part self-recrimination. "Then you do have regrets about last night."

"No, that's not what I meant."

He chose to ignore any further implications and stop any further conversation. He didn't want to delve into it any more than he already had, to truly examine the emotions that so terrified him. "Well, in that case..." He took the glass from her hand and set it on the table, "let's try out the dance floor."

He pulled her into his arms and they began to move to the music. Somehow he had to find some place safe, something between the commitment that so terrified him and doing what he needed to do to make sure he didn't lose her from his life again. If only he knew how to find that safe middle ground.

He closed his eyes and rested his cheek against the top of her head as he held her tightly. Everything he wanted from life was in his arms at that moment, but how would he be able to keep it without making a commitment? His thoughts turned to what would happen following the reception. But he didn't say anything. He continued to hold her in his arms and move to the music as memories of the intensity of their lovemaking flooded his mind.

The music stopped and Jean pulled back from Ry, ending their dance. She glanced at her watch. "It's about time for Susan and Bill to leave for the airport to catch their flight to Paris." She quickly scanned the room. "Apparently everyone is gathering by the door to wish them well, throw rice and vie for the bridal bouquet." She turned her attention to Ry. "If you'll excuse me, I'd better see if Susan needs any help."

Ry held on to her hand for a moment longer, as if reluctant to turn loose of it. He finally brought it to his lips. "Of course. I'll see you in a little bit. Maybe we could go out after the bridal couple make their getaway?"

She hesitated before answering. "Well, I don't know. It's getting late and I am tired." She glanced across the room toward Susan. "I'll talk to you later."

Ry watched as Jean made her way across the large

reception room toward Susan. A sinking feeling settled inside him, a feeling that told him he had not handled things as well as he should have.

Amidst a flurry of activity and delight the bride tossed her bouquet to the crowd, then the happy couple left the reception room. The flowers landed squarely in Jean's hands, almost as if Susan had planned it that way. Jean fought the urge to look at Ry, to see the expression on his face. She didn't want to feel the disappointment if the expression on his face turned out to be anguish rather than pleasure at the unexpected turn of events.

She cradled the flowers in her arms. She would take them home and keep them alive as long as she could, but she knew they would soon fade and then be gone. Was it the same with her relationship with Ry? Would it soon fade until it was only a memory of the passion that once was? She spotted Ry walking toward her. She wasn't feeling very festive anymore.

He eyed the flowers, but was afraid to make mention of them for fear of what they symbolized. Tradition said that whoever caught the bridal bouquet would be the next to marry. A hard band tightened across his chest and a hint of panic set in. He felt as if the walls were closing in around him and he couldn't find his way out.

"About going out..." Jean nervously shifted her weight from one foot to the other. She had too many things to get straight in her mind, not the least of which was her ongoing concern about whether their lapse in good judgment would possibly result in her being pregnant. The fear continued to prey on her mind even though she had tried to shove the unlikely possibility away. "Perhaps some other time. For now, I think I'd better go on home."

His disappointment came out in his words. "Are you sure?"

"Yes. I'm tired and tomorrow morning starts my work week again. I need to get a good night's sleep." She knew she needed sleep, but she suspected it probably wouldn't happen.

"I understand. I'll call you tomorrow after you get home from work. Maybe we could have dinner then? Or if not dinner, maybe we could do something together?"

"Sure, I'll talk to you then."

An overwhelming sense of loss settled inside him as he watched her leave. It was almost like some sort of terrible premonition, as if he was watching her walk out of his life for good.

Five

Jean filled her coffee cup and returned to her desk. Monday was always a busy day for her. As manager of the personnel department at Jarvis Custom Furniture she had numerous reports that had to be filed and all the group health insurance claims to handle. She disliked dealing with the group insurance, but it was part of her job like so many other responsibilities that had been shoved on her. There were days when the personnel department almost seemed like a catch-all location when people didn't know what to do with things.

When she first went to work for Matt Jarvis the company had only thirty employees, but during the ensuing years the company's business had quickly grown to the point where there were now over three hundred full-time employees and another fifty part-time workers. What had been just Jean and one assistant handling all the office functions had become a separate personnel department with six employees in addition to Jean as the manager, which didn't include the accounting department, the purchasing department, several secretaries and a receptionist. Although she appreciated Matt's confidence in her capabilities, she had to admit that there were times when she felt he was taking advantage of her willingness to take on whatever new tasks he threw her way.

She leaned back in her chair, took a sip of her hot coffee and closed her eyes. She had spent a very unsettled night with her thoughts and feelings vacillating between the euphoric memories of the lovemaking she and Ry had shared and her fears about the seeming distance in his voice, all of it compounded by her continued concern about the possibility of being pregnant…remote as she hoped that possibility was. When they had danced at the wedding reception nothing else mattered to her other than the warmth and contentment she found in his arms. But when the physical contact wasn't there her worries and fears would again try to take over. Her uncertainty about Ry's feelings toward her, combined with her growing concern about the possibly of being pregnant, left her confused and uneasy about what to do and what to think.

"Jean, do you have a few minutes?"

Matt Jarvis's voice drew her out of her thoughts. She looked up and her gaze immediately locked on Ry Collier standing next to Matt. The shock stunned her senses and left her momentarily speechless. Her astonishment at seeing Ry matched the surprised expression on his face. A little spark of panic tried to ignite deep inside her. Was this the four week project he had mentioned? Had Matt Jarvis hired him to overhaul Jarvis Custom Furniture? Was Ry Collier in a position to create havoc with her job as well as her personal life?

A sinking feeling settled in the pit of her stomach and

stayed there. Every fiber of her being told her nothing good could come of this. Too many people had tried to control too many aspects of her life. First her grandmother, whose ultra strict, puritanical ways had prevented her from having many friends or participating in any activities while she was in school. Then her husband who demanded from her and never gave of himself, even though she had a full-time job outside the home. And finally her ill-fated love affair following her divorce. The man who at first seemed so perfect had managed to manipulate her into a position where he had isolated her from her friends and had her believing it was to her benefit. All of them had tried to control her life. After she had divorced herself from her husband and her cold grandmother and battled back from the depths of the disastrous relationship that followed, she had vowed she would never allow someone else to have that kind of control over her life again. Was Ry in a position to have that type of control? She tried to swallow her rising trepidation.

"Yes, of course. What can I do for you, Matt?" Her voice didn't contain the confidence she had hoped it would. A nervous anxiety jittered through her body.

"I'd like to introduce you to Ry Collier. He's a consultant I've hired to study all our manufacturing and office procedures and make recommendations for streamlining the department operations, improving our efficiency and instituting some cost-cutting measures. He'll be here for the next four weeks. This week we'll be floating from department to department to check the overall flow and operations, then he'll spend several days in each individual department studying the procedures being used."

Why hadn't Ry told her it was Jarvis Custom Furniture he was evaluating? At least she could have mentally prepared herself for his arrival on the scene. Is that what his attentions over the past week were leading up to? Was his sole purpose in pursuing her nothing more than making sure he had an ally on the inside to support his recommendations? Did he think he could bulldoze his way over her and get what he wanted?

She took a steadying breath. That was ridiculous. She had to rein in her rampaging wild speculations before they got totally out of control. She tried to hide her anxiety. She didn't want Matt Jarvis to know how totally out of control one of his department heads was at that moment. And she certainly didn't want Ry to know how much his appearance at her job had unsettled her.

"I see." She wasn't sure how to handle the fact that she and Ry knew each other. Ry had made no mention of it when Matt had introduced them. She decided to do the same, at least until she could figure out exactly what his angle was in not having confided in her ahead of time. Was her job in jeopardy? Was her career about to be derailed? She needed some answers from Ry—some serious answers.

Matt turned to Ry and extended his hand. "You've met all the department heads now, so if you'll excuse me I have a meeting to attend. I'm going to leave you in Jean's capable hands. Whatever you need, she'll be able to take care of it for you. I'll see you later."

Ry shook hands with Matt. "Thanks." He gave a quick sideways glance at Jean and a wink. "I'm sure she'll be a great help."

Jean watched Matt until he turned the corner and was out of sight. After taking a quick look around her office to make sure no one could hear her, she shot an uncertain stare toward Ry. "What are you doing here? Why didn't you tell me this was the four-week assignment you had accepted?"

He cocked his head and looked at her questioningly, his eyes seeming to search for any hint of what was going on inside her head. "For starters, you didn't ask me. You also didn't tell me you worked for Jarvis Custom Furniture. But either way, why should it make a difference? This is my job, it's what I do for a living and I'm very good at it. I can assure you that I'll treat you and everyone else who works here fairly and impartially. My only request is that our personal situation remain our private business. I don't want anyone else to perceive our knowing each other as something to be either a benefit or detriment to the business at hand."

Something about the way he had said *treat you fairly and impartially* sent a tremor of anxiety through her body. She recalled something he had said, something that was almost a throwaway-type of comment that didn't have any significance at the time. It had to do with his unhappy childhood relationship with his father which had been responsible for his drive to become a success. Did that drive to succeed take precedence over everything else? Was it the reason he was a professed confirmed bachelor? That he didn't have any room in his life for anything that would distract from his drive to succeed at business?

She nervously toyed with her coffee cup, then took another sip before responding. "Yes, I agree that any prior connection between us should remain our business and no one else's, including Matt."

"Good." He sat on the edge of her desk, reached out and ran his fingertips across the back of her hand, then gave it a quick squeeze. "Now, before I get down to work let's take care of one little bit of personal business. I'll pick you up at seven o'clock tonight for dinner. We'll go someplace casual. How does Italian food grab you?"

The second he initiated the physical contact between

them, every fear and concern flew out of her head. Her words came out in a breathless whisper. "Seven will be fine and I love Italian food."

"Good. Now, if you'll excuse me, I need to get to work. As Matt said, this first week I'll be floating around the offices and the plant to observe the overall operational flow. I'll see you later."

Jean watched as he left her office. A sinking nervousness poked inside her. She tried to put it aside. Before she started on her daily routine, she gathered her staff and informed them about Ry's presence and what he would be doing over the next four weeks.

She saw Ry a few times during the course of the day, but it was always on an official business level. He ate in the lunchroom with the rest of the employees, but had chosen a table by himself and appeared to be making notes and working while eating. He seemed so intense, so absorbed in his work. Was this the real Ry Collier? The man who controlled everything around him? Including her future?

About midafternoon Ry retreated to a small office Matt had provided for his use during his four-week stay. He poured a cup of coffee, then settled in at the desk. He made notes on what he had observed, prepared questions he would be asking the next day and began to assimilate the information into the overall structure of his final report.

He leaned back in his chair and took a drink from his coffee cup. It had been a very informative first day. Matt had been right. The company was in desperate need of reorganization and updating of procedures as part of the restructuring. He was certainly going to have his hands full in coming up with an overall restructuring recommendation that wouldn't seem as if he was tearing the entire company apart and rebuilding it. Matt had explained to him that the company had suddenly exploded with success and expanded faster than he could keep up with it, which left him scrambling to meet the needs of his customers and his employees. He had finally come to the realization that even though the company was on sound financial footing, treating the symptoms wasn't going to make things right. He needed a cure and Ry was the person he had chosen to supply it.

Ry's mind turned to thoughts of dinner that night, of being with Jean. So many times during the day he had wanted to pull her into his arms and kiss her, to hold her body tightly against his, to revel in the sensation of her nearness. He knew he had to keep their personal relationship separate from his business interests. Was the temptation of being near her all day without being able to touch her going to be more than he could handle? It was a question that left him uneasy.

He glanced at his watch, then gathered his notes and files. After placing them in his attaché case, he left Jarvis Custom Furniture and returned to his hotel suite. It had been a very enlightening first day on the job, but his thoughts no longer focused on work.

He changed from his suit to jeans and a sweater. With Bill and Susan married and on their honeymoon, he was looking forward to a quiet and relaxing evening with Jean without the underlying stress of the wedding. The surprise of her involvement in his current business project would not put a damper on their evening together. After all, that was only a temporary work assignment and certainly didn't have anything to do with them personally.

He closed his eyes and visualized a quiet little Italian restaurant with a candlelit dinner and then an after-dinner drink in front of the fireplace at Jean's condo—an evening with just the two of them, an evening where they could shut out the world and concentrate only on each other. More than anything he wanted her back in his arms.

Thoughts tried to push into his mind, thoughts about the future, about where he and Jean were headed, but he shoved them aside. Tonight was for the present, not the future. It was for just the two of them. A little twinge of something, he wasn't sure exactly what, shivered up his back. Somewhere along the line his emotions had become so intertwined with his desires that it was becoming more and more difficult to separate them in his mind.

He shook his head to clear away the confusion. He had a couple of hours yet before he would be picking up Jean. He needed to use that time to finish putting his notes in order from the day's observations.

Ry worked quickly and efficiently, making maximum use of his time. As seven o'clock neared, he put his work materials away and left the hotel. Thoughts of Jean filled his mind as he drove to her condo. Tremors of excitement darted through his body as he rang her doorbell. Tonight would be just for the two of them. A moment later she opened the door.

Any and all concerns and apprehensions Jean might have been harboring about both her existing personal and newly initiated work relationship with Ry melted the moment she saw him standing there. He stepped inside, pulled her into his arms, then shoved the door shut with his foot. His mouth instantly found hers, infusing her with a heated kiss that spoke of pure passion plus something else, some hidden longing she couldn't identify. She wrapped her arms around his neck and returned his kiss with an equal amount of passion.

Her senses tingled with a nearly out of control excitement as his tongue brushed against hers. Tremors of anticipation raced through her body recalling the night they had made love. She melted into him. His kiss deepened as he caressed her shoulders. She ran her fingers through his thick hair. Whatever he wanted, she would willingly give.

Then just as she began to entertain thoughts of making love with Ry instead of going out to dinner, a quick surge of panic invaded the sensual fog that surrounded her, pulling her back to reality. She took a step back, breaking off the delicious kiss.

"Ry...I think..." The heated flush of excitement spread across her cheeks and forehead. Everything about him—the sound of his voice, the sight of him, the sensation of his touch, the fire of his kiss—pushed her senses into overload. Somehow she had to be strong. She had to resist the all-too-temping seduction that continually reached out from him and grabbed her whenever they were together. She loved him, but even after they had made love she still didn't have any idea where his emotions stood.

He took a steadying breath, acquiescing to her unspoken words. "You're right. We should probably get going if we're planning on having dinner. Are you ready?"

"Yes, I'm ready." She flashed an engaging smile, partly to cover the inner panic that continued to shove at her, doing battle with her desires. "And I'm hungry."

They drove to a little Italian restaurant in the Pioneer Square Historic District where they were seated in a quiet alcove away from the most crowded part of the room. The candlelight flickered, casting a soft glow across their table. The romantic atmosphere settled over them, providing an intimate closeness.

"Well...." Jean tried to sound casual in spite of the nervousness that continued to jitter inside her. "How did

your first day at work go? Was it what you had anticipated?''

He took her hand. His voice came out as a sexy whisper. ''Let's not waste our time together talking about
stuffy work things.'' He kissed her palm. ''You look
lovely. That blouse is a really good color for you.''

''Thank you.'' Little tremors of delight raced from the
place his lips had touched to every corner of her body,
but it did not negate the tinge of disappointment at the
way he had sidestepped her question.

As much as Jean wanted to ask Ry again about the
first day of his work project, she couldn't seem to find
the right words so that it didn't sound as if she was
prying into his business matters or pushing the subject,
especially after he had changed topics without answering
her initial question. Logically she knew his day-to-day
observations and conclusions weren't anything that he
should be sharing with her, but she also knew his final
recommendations could have a very definite impact on
her job. If his final report showed her department to be
disorganized or poorly run, the results could be disastrous for her.

''You're suddenly very quiet this evening. Is everything okay?'' Ry asked.

He sounded sincere, but she knew he probably didn't
want to hear what was really on her mind. ''I was just
studying the menu. Everything looks so good. As I said
when we left my place, I'm hungry but I can't decide
what to order.'' She looked up at him, making eye contact. ''What looks good to you?''

A sexy smile lit up his handsome face. ''Hmm…that's
a loaded question.'' He squeezed her hand, sending a
heated surge of desire through her body. ''What looks
good to me happens to be sitting right across the table.''

She felt the heated embarrassment spread across her

cheeks. "I was talking about what to order from the menu."

He feigned a sudden understanding of what she had really meant. "Oh…you want to know what I'm going to have for dinner."

They ordered their food. Ry munched on a bread stick as they waited. "How about a movie tomorrow night? We could go out or…" He reached for her hand again, "I could pick up some deli food, rent a video and we could spend the evening at your place."

Once again the sensation of his touch sent waves of excitement through her body. She seemed to lose any and all control over her actions. "That sounds great."

"Any particular movie you'd like to watch?" He reached toward her cheek, running his fingertips softly across her skin.

Her words came out in a breathless whisper. "I'm sure whatever you pick out will be fine."

When their dinner arrived, they took their time eating. They engaged in intimate conversation while savoring the meal. They lingered over coffee and dessert. Following dinner they walked a few doors down the street to a small jazz club where they enjoyed the music. It was nearly midnight when they returned to Jean's condo.

As much as she wanted to invite Ry in, she knew to do so could only lead to one thing. It wasn't that she had misgivings about the night they did make love. Quite the contrary. It would live in her mind as her most cherished memory, but a swirl of confusion about Ry's feelings compounded by her concerns about their not having taken precautions when they made love, had her apprehensive about what to do.

"It was a delightful evening. Thank you for dinner." She noted the quick look of surprise followed by disappointment that darted across his face at her decision to say good-night at the front door.

"It was my pleasure." He leaned forward and placed a tender kiss on her lips. "I'll see you tomorrow."

Ry returned to his car and drove back to the hotel. Troubling thoughts accompanied him. He had the distinct impression that something was bothering Jean, but when he asked her about it she had dismissed his concerns. Was it his imagination? Were his own fears about how much he cared for her causing him to read something into a situation that wasn't there?

As soon as he entered his suite he saw the message light flashing on the phone. There were two messages for him. One was from his office manager in Chicago giving a brief description of a problem and asking him to call her as soon as he got in. The other message sent a cold shudder down his back immediately followed by a quick surge of anger. It was from Marjorie—his ex-wife.

They had been married for only two months and divorced for almost ten years. Even with everything he had been through growing up, his marriage was the single most horrible experience of his life. Marjorie had lied to him, manipulated him into marriage by claiming she was pregnant with his child, then tried to take him to the cleaners in a divorce settlement after he discovered she wasn't pregnant. Fortunately for him, her lies and manipulations were held against her and she was not awarded anything, not even alimony.

He clenched his hand into a fist and tightened his jaw in a hard line. What could she want with him after all these years and more importantly, how did she know where to find him? One thing was for sure, he did not want to talk to her and had no intention of returning her call.

He deleted the messages, checked the time and decided to call his office manager in spite of the fact that it was after midnight in Seattle and much later in Chicago. She had said it was important and she was not prone to exaggeration.

He dialed the number. "Helen? I'm sorry about the late hour, but you said it was important. Did I wake you?"

"No, I was waiting for your call. There's a problem with Glen Windemere."

Ry listened to her report. "I hoped the steps I took would have resolved the problem, but obviously not. I guess this means only one thing. I need to make a quick trip back to Chicago." He grabbed his day planner and studied his schedule. "Let's see…I can fly out Thursday evening after work, take care of the problem on Friday and hopefully be back here Friday evening or Saturday at the latest." He jotted notes in his day planner, then set it aside. "I want you to set up a meeting with those involved for ten o'clock Friday morning. I'll want to meet with my attorney before the ten o'clock meeting. Have him meet me at the office at eight o'clock Friday morning."

"Do you want me to pick you up at the airport?"

"No, there's no need. Thanks for the offer, but I can take a taxi."

As soon as Ry finished his phone conversation, he turned his mind to his work priorities for the rest of the week. He would have Tuesday, Wednesday and Thursday at Jarvis Custom Furniture. He needed to step up his work schedule in order to finish with the first week's work a day early, otherwise it would throw the next three weeks off schedule. Even though it was late, he pulled a file folder from his attaché case and began making notes.

A few minutes later the phone rang.

He grabbed the receiver, a little annoyed at the interruption, yet curious about who it could be at such a late hour. "Hello."

"Is that you Ry darling?"

The syrupy sweet voice cut through him like chalk screeching on a blackboard. Every muscle in his body tensed as he steeled himself against whatever was to come. There wasn't any hint of a gracious manner, courtesy or polite demeanor in his voice. There was, however, an unmistakable harsh edge that clearly conveyed his displeasure at her call.

"What do you want, Marjorie?"

"I just wanted to talk to you, to find out how you are. I'm concerned about you, Ry. You work so hard. Even though we're divorced…a terrible mistake in my opinion…I still care a great deal about you."

His irritation erupted in anger. "Knock it off, Marjorie. You've never cared about anyone or anything except yourself. I don't know what you're trying to sell, but I can assure you I'm not buying. How did you know where to find me?"

"I called your office in Chicago and that nice receptionist told me you were in Seattle. I simply called all the major hotels until I found the one where you were registered."

"Apparently I need to have a chat with my own staff about proper procedure." He made a quick note in his day planner about discussing the problem with Helen, although he suspected it was the temporary agency receptionist filling in for a sick employee who was probably responsible for the slipup.

"So you found me." He made no attempt to hide his annoyance. "What do you want?"

"I want to see you, darling. I thought we could have dinner, maybe talk about our future?"

His anger exploded. "I'm not your darling. And as for the future—we have no future. We didn't have one ten years ago and we certainly don't have one now. We have nothing to talk about and dinner is definitely out of the question."

Ry slammed down the receiver before she had an opportunity to respond. The resentment seethed inside him. He took several deep breaths in an attempt to calm his inner turmoil. The depth of the anger produced by the brief and totally unexpected intrusion by his ex-wife into his life surprised him. Even though he wanted to put the disaster of his short-lived marriage totally out of his mind and dismiss it from his life, he had not been able to do it.

Occasionally he wondered if he had allowed that trauma to impact his relationships with women. Then Jean popped into his mind. Was his fear of what he felt for her the result of his horrible marriage? It was not a new thought, but one that was becoming more difficult to dismiss. It was something he didn't want to dwell on or deal with.

But thoughts of Jean refused to go away—the way she felt in his arms, the earthy heat of her kiss, the night they had made love with such intense passion—it was all burned into his reality and he knew it would stay there forever.

He stared at the file folder on the desk and gave a sigh of resignation. He knew there was no point in trying to get any more work done that night. He would have to revamp his schedule in the morning. Right now his mind was too occupied with thoughts of Jean to concentrate on anything else. He went to bed, but sleep did not come easily. Thoughts continued to swirl around in his mind,

uneasy thoughts about where he and Jean were headed
and what kind of a future they might have.

Jean applied her lipstick and gave her hair a final run
through with the hairbrush. She grabbed her purse, jacket
and car keys, then headed for work.

She had expected Ry to be there early in order to be
present when the employees arrived so he could observe
their start-up procedures for their workday routine. That
seemed to be the type of detail he would be interested
in. To her surprise, he was nowhere in sight. She went
about her business, not sure what to expect from Ry
when he did arrive.

He had pointedly avoided her attempt the previous
night to talk about his observations of his first day on
the job. In retrospect, she knew she was wrong to have
asked about it. He couldn't ethically discuss business
matters with her that he probably hadn't even mentioned
to Matt Jarvis yet. It would be very unprofessional on
his part, but that didn't lessen her anxiety about the situation.

Ry made his appearance about an hour later, said a
respectful and polite hello to everyone, then got down to
business. Jean kept as much of a watchful eye on his
activities as she could while still being able to handle
her own work functions. The day seemed to drag by for
her. She kept looking at the clock wanting it to be time
to leave. Finally five o'clock arrived. She cleaned off her
desk and hurried home.

Jean set the table for dinner, not quite sure what to
put out since she didn't know what food he would be
bringing. Then the doorbell rang. Her heart leaped into
her throat and her pulse raced faster. She rushed to the
door.

Ry stepped inside, placed the sack from the deli and

the videotape on a small table in the entranceway, then quickly pulled her into his arms. He captured her mouth with all the passion he had kept inside during the day, passion that could not be confined any longer. He wanted to scoop her up in his arms and carry her to the bedroom, but after the way she had chosen not to invite him in last night when they had returned from their date he knew he needed to be more cautious. The last thing he wanted was to make her feel rushed or uncomfortable in any way. Or to think that sex was his only interest in her, something that couldn't be further from the truth.

He finally released her. "I've been wanting to do that all day."

Jean self-consciously glanced toward the open front door. "I think we'd better close the door before we give the neighbors and everyone driving down the street any more of a show than we already have." She closed and locked the door.

Ry picked up the food and movie, deposited the videotape on top of the television and continued on to the kitchen. "I wasn't sure what to get. I finally settled on turkey sandwiches and a fresh fruit salad." He pulled the items from the sack along with a bottle of chilled white wine.

He flashed a wry grin as he took a couple of small containers from the sack. "And then my sweet tooth got the better of me and I added a couple of these sinfully delicious desserts."

He turned to her, taking both of her hands in his. "If you set out the food, I'll build a fire in the fireplace."

The evening quickly took on a sensual feel. They ate their dinner and engaged in soft conversation. After eating, Ry poured each of them a glass of wine, then he put the tape in the VCR.

"What movie did you rent?"

"An old one—*Charade* with Cary Grant and Audrey Hepburn."

Her face lit up with delight. "I love that movie. It's one of my all time favorites."

After the movie they settled into the large floor pillows in front of the fireplace and had another glass of wine. Ry put his arm around her shoulders and she snuggled against his body. They silently sipped their wine and watched the flames rhythmically dance across the logs. It was a time of closeness, a personal and intimate feeling that stirred excitement as much as it settled a close contentment over them.

It was a night made for love. For Jean that meant the emotional as much as the physical. If only she knew what that meant for Ry.

But any further thoughts were chased from her mind when he ran his hand up the inside of her pullover shirt, brushed his fingers teasingly across her skin, then unhooked her bra. A soft moan of delight escaped her throat as his mouth came down on hers infusing her with all the passion she had come to associate with Ry Collier.

Ry brushed his tongue against Jean's, exploring the dark recesses of her mouth and relishing the sweet taste that was uniquely hers. She was everything he wanted and more. He cupped her bare breast in his hand, her puckered nipple sending a tingling sensation through his body. His kiss deepened. He wanted it all…he wanted everything…he wanted Jean Summerfield, body and soul.

He pulled her shirt up until it bunched around her neck, then broke the kiss long enough to remove her shirt along with her bra. He dropped the articles to the floor and a moment later his sweater joined the pile. He drew her body against his, reveling in the feel of her bare breasts pressed against his chest. He caressed her shoulders and back, then ran his fingers through her hair.

It didn't take long before all their clothes were scattered across the living room floor. He laid her back on the large floor pillows, taking a moment to watch the way the illumination from the fireplace flickered across her bare skin. A surge of hardened need rushed through his body. He stretched out next to her, purposely taking deep breaths in an attempt to calm his already overexcited desires.

He experienced a warm feeling of utter contentment at just being with her. It spread through him as she caressed his back and ran her foot along his calf. Every place she touched only added to the sensations of his already overstimulated senses.

He nibbled at the corner of her mouth, then rained a series of kisses across her throat, finally drawing her puckered nipple into his mouth. He held it there for a moment, then released the delicious treat. He placed soft kisses between her breasts and slowly continued lower until he reached the downy softness at the apex of her thighs.

Tremors of rapture raced through Jean's body as Ry's hot breath tickled across the sensitive skin of her inner thighs. Then his mouth touched the very core of her femininity, sending waves of ecstasy through her. Her head jerked back into the softness of the large floor pillow. Her fingers trembled as she ran them across the top of his shoulders. She gulped in a lungful of air, then another. She wanted to touch him…she needed to touch him.

He slowly kissed his way up her stomach and between her breasts, ending at the base of her throat. She ran her hand down his ribcage. Just the feel of his skin beneath her fingertips kept her senses in a state of continual excitement. She reached for his hardened arousal, stroking his rigid manhood.

She felt the gasp that escaped his throat and the tremor that moved through his body. Her thoughts quickly faded into oblivion, to be replaced by heated passion. But one last thought remained with her. They had not taken precautions the last time they made love. It had been a very foolish lapse in good sense. She couldn't allow that to happen again.

Before she could say anything, Ry grabbed his jeans and pulled the condom package from the pocket. A few moments later he rolled over on his back and pulled her on top of him. Her legs straddled his hips. She saw the sparkle in the depths of his silver eyes—a silver color that turned to the smoky-gray of passion as he grasped her waist and lifted her to the point where he could lower her on to his hardness.

He closed his eyes as the incredible sensations swept through his body when her heated femininity tightly encased his manhood. As all-consuming as the first time they made love was, this time seemed so much more— more sensual, more exciting, more vital and much more important. There was something he couldn't identify that nearly took his breath away.

He guided her hips into as smooth a rhythm as he was able to maintain. He wanted everything to last forever yet he wanted it all right now. His ragged breathing matched hers. He tried to speak. "Sally Jean…you are so exquisite…so…" He couldn't get out any more words. The upward thrusts of his hips increased, bringing her to a faster pace.

The convulsions started deep inside her and quickly spread through her body. The delicious sensations built one on top of the other as Jean matched Ry's smooth thrusts until she collapsed on top of him, her breasts pressing against his hard chest. She ran her fingers through his thick hair as she gasped for breath. The rhapsody continued to course through the very essence of her life.

Ry teetered on the brink of his control. As much as he wanted this to last, he knew it couldn't. He rolled over on top of Jean, being careful not to break the tangible connection that physically bound them together. He gave a final deep thrust as he wrapped her tightly in his arms. The hard spasms shuddered through his body. He buried his face in her hair as his chest heaved and his pulse raced. He caressed her shoulders as he tried to control his breathing.

Never in his life had he felt as close to a woman as he did to Jean. He flirted with the word love, but couldn't bring himself to truly acknowledge its existence. He knew what he wanted, but feared what he would have to do to have it. He tightened his embrace, holding her body close to his in the hopes that it would give him the emotional strength he needed. He didn't want to let go.

Six

Ry stirred awake when Jean turned over in his arms. He glanced at the glowing numerals reaching out from her nightstand—it was almost six o'clock in the morning. He held her tighter, cupping her breasts in his hands as he snuggled his chest against her back. It had been a glorious night of lovemaking that had touched the very depths of his soul, but a night that had left him even more fearful than he had been before of what was happening.

He kissed her cheek, then whispered in her ear. "Jean, are you awake?" He kissed her cheek again.

"Hmm...." She placed one of her hands on top of his, and ran the other one along his bare thigh, reveling in the warmth of his body touching hers. "Yes, I'm awake."

"The last thing I want to do is untangle this nice cozy place we've found, but it's six o'clock and I need to go back to my hotel so I can get some clean clothes and prepare for work today.''

''You're right, this is definitely cozy.'' It felt so good waking up in Ry's arms. This is the way she wanted it to be, the way she envisioned the future. Was she wanting more than could be?

A hint of a chill invaded her contentment. Work… there was that uneasy situation again. What kind of recommendations would he end up making about her department and how would they impact her job situation? He had dismissed her question last time, but perhaps this would be a better time to pose the question again.

She trailed her fingers across his upper thigh as she ran her foot along the edge of his calf. ''Speaking of work…are things going okay? Is there anything I can do to help?''

''Well.…'' He brushed her fingers away from his leg as he emitted a soft chuckle. ''The first thing you can do to help is stop teasing me. Unless, of course, you think we have time to pursue this to its logical conclusion.'' He ran his hand down her stomach and tickled his fingers through the downy softness. A tremor of delight assailed her senses when his finger penetrated her womanhood.

He nuzzled the side of her neck. ''And I can certainly find the time if you can.''

She took a deep breath in an attempt to calm her spiraling excitement. ''As tempting as your offer is, I'm afraid it's too close to work time. You see, we have this efficiency-expert-type of guy at the office looking over our operation so I need to be on my toes and that includes getting to work on time.''

He wrapped his arms around her and took a calming

breath. "You're right. This may be the place, but it isn't the right time."

Ry threw back the covers and climbed out of bed. "I'll be right back. I'm going to retrieve my clothes from the living room." He hurried downstairs.

Jean slipped out of bed and pulled on her robe. He had done it to her again. He had managed to skillfully sidestep her question about how his work assignment was progressing. Intellectually she understood his decision not to discuss it with her, but emotionally the matter left her uneasy.

Her gaze fell on the opened condom packet on the nightstand, the mate to the discarded packet in the living room. Ry had obviously anticipated their making love and had come prepared. But then her thoughts turned to the first time they had made love. Continuing to swirl in the back of her mind was the fact that they had not taken precautions. She tried to tell herself that her fears were unfounded, that she couldn't possibly be pregnant, but she had not been able to convince herself of that.

She knew it didn't do any good to dwell on the possibility, but she couldn't help it. Another week and she could have something real to worry about rather than baseless fears. If her period hadn't materialized by next week, then she would get one of those home pregnancy tests. She took a calming breath. It was ridiculous to put herself through this mental torture. She was allowing her fears to run wild and she needed to rein them in before they got totally out of control.

When Ry returned to the bedroom, he wore his briefs, had pulled on his jeans although he had not zipped them up and was carrying his sweater, shoes and socks. He dropped everything on the bed, then folded Jean into his embrace. She wrapped her arms around his waist and he held her for several minutes without saying anything. He ran his fingers through her hair, nestled her head against his shoulder and rested his cheek against her head.

"I probably need to get in the shower and get ready for work," Jean finally said.

A teasing grin tugged at the corners of his mouth. "If it wasn't for the time growing later and later, I'd suggest that we conserve water by showering together, but I'm afraid lathering each other's body would not be conducive to hurrying."

"I think you're right," she said, laughing.

Ry sighed and finally turned loose of her. He placed a tender and loving kiss on her lips, then finished getting dressed. He took her hand in his. "I'd better get out of here. I'll see you later."

Jean walked downstairs with Ry and watched as he backed out of her driveway. She closed the front door and went upstairs to her bathroom. A few minutes later she stood under the hot steamy spray of the shower. She loved him…she loved him so much. What would happen if she turned out to be pregnant? How would he react to the news? As much as she wanted a family of her own, this wasn't the way she wanted it to happen.

A cold shiver darted through her body in spite of the warm steam that surrounded her. She had never been so happy and so frightened all at the same time.

Ry glanced at the clock on Jean's nightstand. "I'm sorry I need to leave so early, but I have a ton of work to do before tomorrow morning." He placed a final loving kiss on her lips, then rose from the edge of the bed and went downstairs. Each workday had become more and more difficult for him, being around Jean and not being able to touch her. But after work hours…well, that was a different story, just as it had been the night before.

Each time he was near her it became more and more difficult to leave. Thoughts of Jean occupied all his waking hours and had even invaded his dreams. And it left him confused and very fearful about what to do and what the future held.

As soon as he was in his suite, he pulled out his attaché case and started to work. His emergency trip to Chicago tomorrow right after work would cost him a day on the Jarvis Furniture job. He couldn't allow his other business concerns to interfere with this work project. It meant he would need to put in longer hours, which he was certainly willing to do. Hard work had never scared him.

He leaned back in his chair. The only thing that truly scared him was his feelings for Jean Summerfield and where they were taking him. His wandering thoughts were interrupted by the ringing phone.

"Hello."

"Ry, darling. I've been calling you all evening. I'm glad you finally got back."

He let out a sigh, part exasperation and part irritation at the identity of the caller. "What do you want now, Marjorie? And make it brief, I'm very busy."

"I want to see you, Ry. You know, maybe have a drink and talk. Get to know each other again."

"I already know you better than I want to. I'm not interested in any new information."

Ry hung up the phone. The anger seethed inside him. How dare she think she could just waltz back into his life, especially after what she had done—lying to him to manipulate him into a marriage he didn't want. He took a calming breath and forced his attention to the notes he had removed from a file folder. He read them, then sorted the notes into various categories. A knock at his door drew his concentration away from the task at hand.

Total shock invaded his reality when he opened the door and saw Marjorie. He quickly recovered his composure and stood his ground. He refused to move aside so she could come in, but he could not contain his anger.

"What the hell are you doing here?"

"Now, Ry…" She managed to slip past him to enter the parlor room of his suite. She closed the door. "Is that any way to talk to your wife?"

"Ex-wife, Marjorie… Ex-wife. As in no longer and not ever again." His words came out in a harsh tone clearly showing his anger and bitter resentment. "You told me you were pregnant with my child so that I'd do the honorable thing and marry you even though I didn't love you. Then I found out you weren't pregnant at all and never had been. You lied to me and manipulated me in the worst possible way. There is nothing you can say or do that is of any interest to me. Now take yourself back to whatever hellhole you crawled out of and leave me alone. I don't want to see you and I don't want to talk to you."

"I flew to Seattle just to be with you. You don't want to see me?" She took off her coat and let it drop to the floor, revealing her nude body. She smiled coyly. "Not even if it's all of me?"

He picked up her coat and tossed it at her. "Especially if it's all of you. Now get out of my life and stay out!"

"Apparently this is a bad time for you, darling. I'll be in town for a few days and am staying right here at this hotel. Let's have breakfast tomorrow morning. I can order from room service and we can have a nice private talk away from the hotel coffee shop."

"Hell will freeze over first. You can stay in town as long as you want. I'm returning to Chicago tomorrow." He watched as she stood there, making no attempt to put on her coat. He reached for the door. "You'd better cover up or else you'll be in the hallway giving everyone a good look."

A minute later he had ejected Marjorie from his room. He didn't know what her game was this time, but he was not going to allow her to manipulate him into playing it. The tension knotted in the pit of his stomach. He looked down and saw that his hands were tightly clenched into hard fists. He unclenched them and took several deep, calming breaths, but it was no good. He closed his eyes and took another deep breath, held it for a few seconds, then slowly exhaled. He couldn't allow her to intrude into his life, to push the buttons that brought out the worst in him—to be able to control his anger and resentment by her mere presence.

He had work to do and that was where he needed to put his efforts. To waste energy on being angry with Marjorie over something that happened ten years ago was definitely counterproductive. But he couldn't focus. And it wasn't Marjorie and her irritating antics that had him distracted. Marjorie's unexpected visit had made him even more aware of how much he wanted to be with Jean, how special she was, how much he wanted a serious relationship with her.

He forced his attention back to work. After two hours he had come up with a restructured schedule that would make up for the day he would be losing at Jarvis Furniture. He glanced at his watch. It was late. He put his work materials away and went to bed, but it was a night that vacillated between both romantic and erotic dreams of Jean and troubled concerns about the real reason for Marjorie's sudden reappearance in his life.

The next morning he arrived at work early so he could observe the arrival and start-up procedures the employees used. This would be his last day of general observations before moving on to his scrutinization of the individual departments.

He was on his second cup of coffee by the time Jean arrived at work. He closed her office door so they could have some privacy. "I have to go back to Chicago tonight—"

He saw the shocked expression that blanketed her features and immediately moved to correct her misconceptions. "No…just for a day or two. I have an emergency business problem that requires my immediate attention in my office. I'll be leaving this evening and will try to be back tomorrow night, but I'm afraid it will more likely be sometime Saturday afternoon before I can be back in Seattle."

He glanced toward the office door, then pulled her into his arms. "I'll miss you. Would it be okay if I stop by on my way to the airport this evening? Maybe around six o'clock?"

"Yes, I'd like that."

He placed a soft kiss on her lips, then straightened up and became all business again. "Now, I need to go back to work."

The day passed surprisingly quick for Jean, but whenever she had a lull her thoughts would immediately turn to Ry and what the future held for her. The surge of panic that instantly swept through her when Ry said he was returning to Chicago…well, that certainly said it all. She was hopelessly in love with him and couldn't imagine what life would be like without Ry Collier.

Then a far greater concern shoved aside those thoughts. What if she really was pregnant? How would she tell Ry? What would he say and do? She counted on her fingers how many days it had been since they had made love without taking precautions and calculated when her period should begin. How soon could she use a home pregnancy test? She didn't know anything about them. Perhaps she should stop by the drugstore on her way home from work. She didn't need to buy one, but she could read the information on the package which would hopefully tell her how soon she could take the test and have it be viable. She tried to shake away the disturbing thought, but it wouldn't totally leave her consciousness. With each passing day it had become a more disturbing thought. She forced herself back to work.

Ry left Jarvis Custom Furniture at about four o'clock and Jean departed work an hour later. She almost pulled into the parking lot of the drugstore on her way home, but at the last moment changed her mind. She was being foolish. She couldn't be pregnant, she simply couldn't be. She gathered her determination and confidence. She was obviously allowing her anxiety to get too much of a foothold and she needed to put an immediate stop to it.

She took care of a couple of other errands and finally arrived home a little before six o'clock. As soon as she had changed clothes her doorbell rang. She opened the door to Ry.

"I only have a few minutes. I just didn't want to leave without seeing you. I have a quick meeting with my attorney first thing in the morning, then a meeting later in the morning at my office. It's a meeting that could go all day and even carry over to Saturday."

Jean wasn't sure what to think or say. "Are…are you

in some sort of trouble? Is there anything I can do to help?"

He wrapped his arms around her and flashed a confident smile. "No, it's nothing like that. Just a business problem that I thought was resolved, but it reared its ugly head again. It's a nuisance, nothing more. Everything will be fine. I'll give you a call when I get back." He placed a soft kiss on her lips. "Let's go somewhere Saturday night…whatever you want to do."

"That sounds good to me. I'll see you then."

Ry stayed about fifteen minutes longer, putting off his trip to the airport until the last possible minute. Jean watched as he drove down the street. Even though he said he'd only be gone for a day or two, she suddenly felt so alone. What would happen in three weeks when his work assignment was over? Would he be gone for good? Was it possible to carry on a long distance relationship? Relationship…there was that word again. Did they have a relationship beyond the here and now? She didn't know. It was a realization that left her both sad and uneasy.

She did a few things at home that evening, chores that had been put on hold because most of her spare time over the past two weeks had been spent with Ry. She went through the motions, but her mind wasn't with it. All her thoughts were centered on Ry and what type of future they had. And never far from the forefront of her thoughts was the possibility of her being pregnant—a notion that had at first been remote but had became more frightening each time she thought of it.

Jean's Friday workday was finally over and it was officially the weekend. She looked around her living room. It seemed so quiet and empty. Would Ry be back that evening or would it be Saturday before she saw him? Her thoughts were interrupted by her doorbell. She opened the door to find a woman she'd never seen before, but one who didn't look as if she was selling anything or taking a survey.

"Yes? May I help you?"

An uneasy feeling settled in the pit of Jean's stomach in response to the way the other woman was looking her over, as if checking her out. When the woman didn't respond to her question, Jean spoke up. "Who are you and what do you want?"

"I'm Marjorie Collier...Mrs. Ryland Collier." She scrutinized Jean again. A cruel and sardonic laugh escaped her throat. "Humph...Ry usually has better taste than this. I guess you must have been handy and *very* accommodating."

The shock almost knocked Jean's legs out from under her. Her heart pounded in her chest and she was momentarily speechless. "You're...you're Mrs. Ryland Collier? Ry's married?"

"As if you didn't know."

"I didn't know." A sick feeling churned in the pit of Jean's stomach as her insides twisted into knots. Not again. This couldn't be happening to her...not again. She had been down this road before and now she was going to have to tread that same path one more time? The relationship she had following her divorce had seemed as if it was leading somewhere...until she had been confronted by the man's wife. The realization that he had lied to her about being married had been far more devastating than her miserable marriage.

Jean forced the horrible memories aside, finally making room for her logical thought process to return. Susan had specifically mentioned at the prewedding get-acquainted party that Ry was single. Whoever this woman was, she certainly couldn't be Ry's wife.

Jean leveled a steady gaze at Marjorie even though it was far removed from the almost unbearable panic shooting around inside her. "And I still don't know that he's married. I'm afraid that it will take a lot more than some stranger standing at my door to convince me of that."

"Really?" Marjorie opened her purse and produced her driver's license showing her name as Marjorie Collier. "I think this should satisfy any doubts you have."

"The only thing that will satisfy me is hearing it directly from Ry in person."

"I guess he didn't even bother to tell you. He went back to Chicago yesterday."

Jean's outer manner remained confident and defiant, her words said as a challenge. "If he's gone home, then why are you here rather than in Chicago?"

The sarcasm dripped from Marjorie's words. "It's just one of the little chores I always have to do. I'm the one who cleans up after Ry's numerous little escapades."

"I don't know who put you up to this, but there's nothing here that needs cleaning up. Go peddle your malicious trash somewhere else!" Jean slammed the door in Marjorie's face. Her insides twisted into hard knots to the point where she felt physically ill. Her legs turned wobbly and her hands trembled. She grabbed the edge of the fireplace mantel for support. Could it possibly be true? Had Ry been deceiving her from the moment Susan introduced them at the party? Had he managed to fool Susan and Bill, too?

She swallowed the sick feeling rising in her throat. It couldn't be true. It simply couldn't. Whoever this Marjorie Collier was and whatever her game was, she

couldn't be Ry's wife. But as much as she wanted to
believe her own words, Marjorie's claim had left a hole
in her belief of what was true and what wasn't.

Jean sank into the softness of the large floor pillows
in front of the fireplace, the same pillows where she and
Ry had made love so passionately just a few days ago.
She thought back over the past two weeks, of all the
time they had spent together. Was this how it would all
end? Self-doubt flooded through her consciousness. Ry
told her he would be back, but would he?

The hotel—certainly he wouldn't pack up everything
he had brought for a five week stay and check out just
to be gone one night or two at the most. She could call
the hotel and see if he was still registered. She dismissed
the idea as quickly as it had come to her. It was a ridiculous thought. It would be like spying on him. She tried
to pull her confidence together. Of course Ry would be
back. He had a job to finish at Jarvis Custom Furniture.
Whoever this Marjorie was, she obviously didn't know
that his work assignment in Seattle still had three weeks
to go.

The logical realization went a long way toward easing
her mind, but did not completely drive away the doubts
Marjorie had planted there. What if he really was married? In an almost involuntary action her hand went to
her abdomen. And what if she was pregnant with his
child? What had been a simple fear had suddenly become
a very complex one. If what Marjorie said was true, then
it would no longer be a matter of how to tell Ry if she
was pregnant. It would be a matter of whether to tell him
at all.

The troublesome thoughts continued to circulate
through her mind. Her heart wanted to believe that Marjorie was just some kind of nut, but that didn't explain

how Marjorie knew to come to her front door. How would she have known that Jean's relationship with Ry was far more than merely business? Would Ry have told Marjorie about their relationship? Told Marjorie where she lived? And how would she have known that Ry flew back to Chicago yesterday? She shook her head as she tried to bring some control to her escalating fears.

If she truly loved Ry she should trust him, but she had been down that road before. A shiver of trepidation accompanied by the memory of the pain she had suffered told her what she didn't want to know. Her insides twisted into knots. She didn't want to repeat the horrible inevitability although she knew she was already far too emotionally involved with Ry to escape unscathed. Remembrances of her ill-fated relationship with a married man filled her thoughts.

Following her divorce she had become involved with a man she thought was absolutely wonderful. He doted on her, treated her with kindness and affection. It was so different from her miserable marriage. She had probably become so deeply involved with him to the point of it being an intense affair because he was so different from her ex-husband. She believed she had finally found the happiness that had eluded her all her life.

But she had been so wrong. She even accepted the way he had distanced her from her friends so that he was the primary person in her life.

She would never forget that awful day when his wife came to her door, much in the same way as Marjorie had that evening. The woman informed Jean that she had been dating a married man—her husband. She showed Jean pictures of the two of them with their three children, the most recent photo having been taken just two weeks prior. And on top of that, his wife was obviously pregnant.

Jean was mortified and embarrassed. She didn't know what to say to the woman other than to repeat over and over again that she had no idea he was married. When Jean confronted her lover with the information, he behaved in a very blasé manner saying his marriage didn't have anything to do with them and their relationship. That terrible moment still lived inside her. The hurt had surged through her long after the affair was over, while her anger seethed inside. First a disastrous marriage, then a cruel betrayal by a man she trusted and believed in.

It had been a lesson learned the hard way, but one well learned. She had vowed to never lose her heart again, never to allow anyone to be able to hurt her the way she had been hurt. So, how could she explain the predicament she was in at that moment? Once again she had been confronted by a woman claiming to be the wife of a man she loved, with the added stress this time of the possibility that Jean might be pregnant with his child. Tears welled in her eyes. She quickly blinked them away and gathered her determination. Whatever happened, she had to take responsibility for her own actions and for her life. Then the tears slowly trickled down her cheeks accompanied by a cold chill.

What if Ry really was married? How would she ever be able to trust anyone again? And what would her life be like if she had to spend the rest of her years always wondering if someone was lying to her? And if she was pregnant…how could she raise a child if her entire life was built on not trusting anyone? What kind of values were those to pass on to a child?

The sick churning in the pit of her stomach tried to

work its way up her throat. She suddenly felt so very alone…alone and afraid.

She wanted to be angry—angry with Ry for betraying her and angry with herself for once again falling for the wrong man. But the anger refused to materialize. All she felt was the pain.

Seven

Jean stared at the results of the home pregnancy test. Her insides twisted into hard knots and her throat tightened. She shook her head. There had to be some sort of mistake. It couldn't be true, it just couldn't. Regardless of how concerned she had been about this, how much it had occupied her thoughts, the unbelievable results still shocked her and caught her unprepared for the reality. She had taken three tests and all three said the same thing. She was pregnant with Ry's child.

She had spent a night of turmoil after Marjorie left. Dark thoughts and fears swirled through her dreams. To be pregnant would create enough problems, but if Ry was married her problems would be multiplied to the point where she wasn't sure how she would be able to handle them. Had Ry been deceiving her all along? Was the story he told her about what had happened with the prom fifteen years ago nothing more than empty words to appease her? Had she been handed the final and most devastating humiliation and betrayal?

She had gone to the drugstore as soon as she woke Saturday morning. She looked over all the different types of home pregnancy tests, reading the information printed on the outside of the boxes. She had chosen three tests from three different manufacturers.

She stared at the used paraphernalia scattered on the bathroom counter from all three tests she had taken. All three had produced the same results. Her throat tightened. Her mouth felt dry as cotton. Perhaps the tests were flawed. It was one of the newer types of tests that said she could get ninety-nine percent accurate results four days sooner than the tests that required her to wait until the day after her period was supposed to start.

Ninety-nine percent wasn't one hundred percent. There was still that one percent margin for error. She would wait four days and try it again, this time choosing different tests. She knew she was grasping at straws. Deep down inside she suspected the outcome would be the same. And if it was she would make an appointment with her doctor, but that wouldn't change the truth.

Jean wandered aimlessly into the living room and sank into the couch. She was so confused. She didn't know what or who to believe. She desperately needed to see Ry. She stared at the phone trying to silently will it to ring, to have the caller be Ry telling her he was back in town. He would be able to explain everything. He would make everything okay. A cold chill shot up her spine. Explaining Marjorie was one thing, but that wouldn't fix the fact that she was pregnant. That wouldn't change how drastically her life was about to be altered, and possibly Ry's, too.

She stared at the phone, but nothing happened. It remained silent…a silence that soon became deafening and all-too-painful to endure. The sick churning returned to the pit of her stomach, then tried to work its way up her throat. She couldn't be experiencing morning sickness. It was definitely too soon for that. It had to be stress— stress combined with fear and panic. She went to the bathroom to clean up the pieces of the pregnancy tests. Her hand visibly shook as she reached for an empty box. The sick churning increased. She swallowed several times in an attempt to make it go away.

She gathered her determination and cleaned up the mess. She tried to concentrate on other things, but nothing helped. Saturday was already half gone without a call from Ry. Jean had picked up the phone several times to call the hotel, but each time had replaced the receiver without dialing. What was nervous anxiety had turned into full-blown panic.

She tried to pull her logical thoughts together. She needed to deal with this unexpected turn of events one step at a time. First she had to talk to Ry about Marjorie, about what Marjorie had told her. She could not address the pregnancy until his marital status was clarified. In her heart she knew it couldn't be true, he couldn't be married. But it was an issue she could not ignore, the repeat of a horrible episode from her past she thought she would never have to live through again.

She picked up a book and tried to concentrate on reading, but it was no use. She glanced at the clock every few minutes only to be disappointed at the way time seemed to be standing still.

It was almost six o'clock that evening before the ringing phone broke the uncomfortable silence that surrounded her. Her heart pounded as she grabbed the receiver. It had to be Ry…it just had to be.

"Hello."

"Hi. I just arrived at the hotel."

Nothing had ever sounded so good to her as he did at that moment. She tried to force a calm to her voice, to keep her rampaging anxiety and panic under control until she could sit down with Ry face-to-face and talk this out.

"I…uh…was beginning to think you might not be coming back." She emitted a chuckle in an attempt to keep the conversation casual, hoping it didn't sound as strained as it felt. "But then I remembered you still had three weeks of your work assignment before you were finished with the contract."

He allowed a soft laugh. "Well, I have to admit that I didn't think I'd be gone this long. The meeting ended up being all day Friday and most of today before we had everything resolved. I left the wrap up details to my attorney and my office manager and caught the next flight back to Seattle."

His voice turned serious. "Have you already had dinner? Is it too late to do whatever it is you had planned for tonight?"

Plans for Saturday night—between Marjorie's unsettling visit and the disturbing results of the pregnancy tests, she had completely forgotten that he had asked her if she would make plans for them for Saturday night.

"I didn't make any plans. I was afraid you might not be back in time to do something that required a specific start time and I didn't know how tired you'd be. So, the evening is open."

"Well, you're right. I am a little tired. Have you eaten yet?"

"No…I…uh…I had a late lunch." Was he trying to get out of seeing her that night? She drew in a deep breath. Or was she letting her imagination run away with her again, allowing her own anxieties to influence reality?

"I'd like to see you tonight. Is it okay if I come over? I have a few things to unpack, but I could be there in about forty-five minutes. Would that be okay?"

"Yes, I'll see you then."

Jean replaced the receiver, allowing her hand to linger on it for a moment before turning loose. She desperately needed to calm the trepidation that seemed to have claimed every corner of her existence. She tried to get her thoughts straight, to put things in some sort of logical order before he arrived.

The first thing she needed to do was tell him about Marjorie's visit and her claim that they were married. Until that was resolved there was no use in attempting to tell him she might be pregnant. In fact, there was no use in mentioning it at all until she was sure. A cold chill settled over her. It matched the icy fear that churned inside her.

It couldn't be true, it just couldn't be…none of it, not Ry being married and not her being pregnant. It was all some kind of dreadful nightmare. She would wake up and find that everything was blissful and happy. She loved Ry. Why couldn't that be enough to make everything else all right?

The tears began to well in her eyes. She quickly brushed them away, then went to the bathroom and splashed cold water on her face. She had to make sure her eyes didn't look red and puffy. She didn't want Ry to immediately suspect that something was wrong. She wanted to be able to tell him in her own way and her own time frame.

It seemed like forever before she heard the doorbell

even though it had been less than an hour. She rushed to the door. A moment later Ry stepped inside and pulled her into his arms. The moment he wrapped her in his embrace she immediately felt so safe and secure, as if nothing could ever hurt her. She didn't want to ever lose the sensation. She wrapped her arms around his waist.

He caressed her shoulders and stroked her hair. It felt so good to have her back in his arms. He had not realized how empty his life was until he spent Friday night alone, rambling around in his large house. He had used so much energy building his fortune and making a success of his career that he hadn't taken the time to discover what was missing from his life. After his horrible experience with marriage he had convinced himself that to be tied down to one woman in a permanent relationship, whether married or not, was to take away from him any choices and freedom he might have. It would be a fate worse than death.

Jean had made him realize how wrong he had been, how much he needed someone to make his life complete. And that special someone was Jean Summerfield. His high school friend from fifteen years ago had become the most important person in his life. He didn't want to think about a future without her.

His words came out slightly husky. "I know I've only been gone for two days, but I sure missed you."

"I missed you, too."

He lowered his head and captured her mouth with a kiss that spoke of tenderness and caring, then it quickly escalated into the heated passion that had been stored away for two days. Her earthy response matched everything churning inside him, all the incendiary desires that had been pent-up while he was in Chicago.

He caressed Jean's shoulders, then ran his fingers

through her silky hair. She melted into his sensual touch and the magic of his kiss. So many thoughts circulated through her mind, things they had to talk about, things that could set the tone for the future she hoped they had together. Or a bigger fear, things that could spell the end to any future they might have had. Her anxiety level rose to match her heated desires. Then Ry twined his tongue with hers and all her thoughts and fears evaporated into a cloud of euphoria…all but one. Still pushing at her consciousness was the panic that told her she had to find the words to tell Ry she was pregnant—words she knew could spell disaster.

Jean glanced at the clock on the nightstand. It was only eight-thirty. The move from her front door to her bedroom two hours ago had been spontaneous and immediate. And now she laid wrapped in his embrace as they snuggled beneath the blankets. Everything about him excited her beyond what she thought was possible. But it was so much more than just the physical. He touched her soul the way no one else ever had. His arms tightened around her sending a wave of pleasure coursing through her veins.

Now that the urgency of their lovemaking had been satiated and the sensual mood had settled into a warm glow of contentment, her thoughts returned to the problems that had been shoved aside, but definitely not forgotten. And first on that list was Marjorie. A nervous twinge told her how much she dreaded having to confront him with what had happened. In her heart she didn't believe it, but she knew the matter had to be brought out in the open and addressed. Even if it wasn't true, Ry needed to be aware of Marjorie's attempts to undermine him.

Jean took a steadying breath to calm her increasing level of trepidation, spurred on by the awkwardness of what she was about to say. She could not put it off any longer. She placed her hands on top of his, relishing the warmth and intimacy of their bare skin touching along the length of their bodies—a closeness that she hoped would still be there after she asked him about Marjorie.

"Ry?" Her apprehension rose sharply.

"Mmm...yes?"

"Uh...something happened yesterday evening...and... uh..."

His senses jumped to full alert. Something was wrong, very wrong. He heard it in her voice. He raised up on one elbow so that he could clearly see her face. He placed his fingertips beneath her chin and lifted until he could look into her eyes. What he saw there sent a jolt of fear through him.

"Jean, what's the matter?" A touch of panic invaded his reality. What had been blissful contentment just moments ago had turned into an unsettling concern. "What happened?"

"Well—" she swallowed and glanced nervously around the room before regaining eye contact with him "—I had a visitor yesterday right after I got home from work."

Ry furrowed his brow in confusion as he shook his head. "You had a visitor? I don't understand. Who was it? What was troubling about this visit?" He didn't know where the conversation was headed, but it left him decidedly uneasy. "Are you all right?"

"It was...uh..." She had to look away. She couldn't hold his eye contact any longer. "It was a woman who said her name was...uh...Marjorie Collier." She felt his muscles immediately tense into tight knots. Her heart sank and an uncomfortable awareness welled inside her. He obviously knew the name.

His words were carefully measured. He spoke through a clenched jaw, any emotion he felt obviously being held back and carefully controlled. "Marjorie was here?"

Jean took another breath, then plunged quickly into what she had to say before she lost her nerve. "She said she was your wife, that I had been dating a married man. She said this behavior was common for you, that you usually had these short-term affairs whenever you were out of town on a job, that I was just one more of many. She also said you'd gone back to Chicago and indicated that you wouldn't be returning to Seattle. She claimed she usually cleaned up after these flings of yours and that was what she was doing at my door."

A cold shudder ran through her body followed by an almost uncontrollable trembling. Time seemed to hang in the air forever without Ry saying or doing anything. She couldn't stand the silence any longer. She looked up at him. His features were contorted into an angry mask. She had never seen anyone as angry as he appeared. The muscles in his face were set into hard lines, his jaw clenched so tight that it was almost as if he was afraid to speak for fear of what he might say. And his eyes, they were dark and stormy—and very frightening.

Her voice quavered as she spoke. "Ry?" She reached out until her fingertips touched his cheek. It felt hard as stone. She forced the words, not sure if she should say anything or not. "I don't understand what's going on. Talk to me…please? What's happening? Who is this Marjorie? How did she know to come here?"

His arms tightened around her, but it was not a forceful or angry move. It was as if he were reaching out for some sort of confirmation of what they had together, trying to draw some comfort and assurance from her. The sensation sent a little wave of relief through her, but didn't answer her questions.

Ry gulped in several deep breaths in an attempt to bring some sort of calm and rationale to his shattered composure. He tried to make his voice sound calm and under control, a far cry from the chaos that churned inside him. "Marjorie came here? She claimed to be my wife?"

"Yes. Obviously, this is someone you know. Who is she?" Jean paused, then said the words that she dreaded, the words that were so difficult for her. "Ry, are you married? Is…is Marjorie your wife?"

He sank back into the softness of the bed, drawing her body close to his and continuing to hold on to her. "No, I'm not married. Marjorie is my ex-wife. We were married for two months and have been divorced for almost ten years."

His words shocked her. He had mentioned a brief marriage, but she never suspected that it would have been that short. She blurted out her response before she could censor herself. "You were only married for two months?"

The anger and bitterness surrounded his words. "Two months was more than enough—it was a lifetime. The marriage should never have happened."

She waited, but he didn't elaborate. It was as if he didn't have any intention of talking about how or why he had married and why the marriage had been so short-lived. She suddenly felt as if she was prying into something that was none of her business.

A moment later, Ry continued with what he had been saying before she interrupted him. "Other than to say that Marjorie is very devious and manipulative and I wouldn't put anything out of the realm of possibility where she is concerned, I can't explain how she knew about you or where you live.''

"But why would she do such a thing? Why would she come here and claim that the two of you were married and accuse me of dating her husband as if I were a home wrecker who was beneath contempt?''

"She's a selfish, mean, manipulative and vindictive woman who doesn't care about anything or anyone other than herself. She called me a few days ago…first time I've heard from her since the divorce. She said she wanted to get together to talk over old times. I told her we didn't have any old times to talk over and I didn't want to see her. I had assumed that would be the end of it, but obviously I was wrong.''

He took a calming breath before continuing. "Apparently that spurred her into action and she caught a flight to Seattle. Wednesday night when I got back to my hotel room, she surprised me with an appearance at my door. I told her she was wasting her time and that I was returning to Chicago the next day. Once again I apparently made a bad assumption that telling her I was going back to Chicago would be her cue to leave Seattle. She obviously had other plans. She must have been in Seattle for a while before she made her presence known to me.''

He stroked Jean's skin and ran his fingers through her hair, then held her tightly in his embrace. "Please believe me, Jean. It's the truth.'' He paused and took a deep breath, slowly expelling it. "The only thing Marjorie means to me is disaster and problems. This is the first time I've seen or heard from her in almost ten years, ever since that glorious day our divorce was final.''

She heard the bitterness in his voice and the underlying resentment that he couldn't hide. Whatever had happened to cause the marriage to be such a short one obviously still lived in a volatile place locked deep inside him, an emotion that had manifested itself in his comment about being a confirmed bachelor.

"I believe you. I knew there had to be some sort of logical explanation for what had happened. I told her I would only believe you were married if I heard it from you personally, then I slammed the door in her face."

"I'm so sorry, Jean." He placed a tender kiss on her lips. "I'm so sorry that she put you through this. Are you all right? Is there anything I can do?"

"I'm fine." A shiver of anxiety darted through her body. *Except, of course, for being pregnant with your child.* "I just needed to hear from you that it wasn't true, that you weren't married and cheating on your wife." Yes, everything was settled except for confronting him with the news that he was going to be a father. She was not ready to tackle that situation...not yet. She had to wait until she was positive about being pregnant, not just ninety-nine percent sure. She needed to wait a few more days to take another home test and if the results confirmed the earlier test, then she would see her doctor. She had made her decision. She would not say anything to him until she had it confirmed by a doctor. A sinking feeling told her it wasn't going to be that easy.

Ry suddenly sat up, drawing her attention away from her inner turmoil. He stared at her, as if trying to get his thoughts together. "Did Marjorie ever address you by name?"

She looked at him quizzically as she furrowed her brow in concentration. "No, I don't think so. She simply appeared at my front door, told me who she was and made her accusations."

"Then it's possible that she doesn't really know who

you are, only where you live. And if that's true it means she probably has no idea where you work or what my work assignment is here. So she must have followed me from the hotel to your condo one evening.''

He again pulled her into his arms. His words were soft, some of the bitterness had gone from his voice. ''I'm glad you stood up to her the way you did. That took a lot of courage on your part. It probably took the wind out of her sails and left her a little unsure about what to do. In fact…'' He reached for the phone and dialed a number.

''Who are you calling?''

''I'm calling the hotel to see if she's still registered. Hopefully your response sent her to the airport. That and the fact that I told her I was leaving but didn't say it was only for a day or two.''

Ry's phone conversation was short and succinct. Marjorie had checked out of the hotel. A wave of relief settled over him. Between his firm stand with Marjorie and Jean's equally defiant attitude with her, maybe she had gotten the message and decided to abandon whatever plan had been circulating through her devious little mind. Ry again pulled Jean into his arms and held her tenderly.

''Ry, do you think she could be stalking you?'' Her voice quavered. ''Or me?''

''I truly believe Marjorie has a screw loose somewhere, but I don't think she'd resort to stalking. I don't think she'll be bothering you again.'' He placed a tender kiss on her lips. ''I feel so bad about you being subjected to this.''

He stroked her hair and nestled her head against his shoulder. ''Are you all right? Do you have any questions you want to ask me? If you do, please go ahead. I don't want you to be bothered by anything, especially if it can be easily explained and dealt with.''

Would it be all right if she asked him about his marriage, about why it lasted only two months? No, she would not pry. He hadn't volunteered the information when the subject was open so she wouldn't pursue it. Should she tell him about the horrible experience from her past? About the way the confrontation with Marjorie was not a new experience for her? How she was once before confronted by an irate wife who accused her of dating a married man? About the fact that the truth had devastated her?

A wave of sadness washed over her. No, she would not tell him. It was a personal matter that she would keep to herself. Perhaps at some future date when she was more sure of what type of relationship she and Ry had, when she was more secure about his feelings.

She tried to switch to a confident manner. ''In my heart I knew you couldn't be married, but I had to ask.''

''I'm glad you did. I don't want another fifteen years to pass before an unfortunate incident is explained. I don't want any other obstacles standing between us.''

Obstacles standing between us…he had said the words, but he wasn't sure exactly what he had meant by them or for that matter exactly why he had said them. Had he allowed his true feelings to seep through? Had he said more than he intended?

Ry tightened his arms around Jean, reveling in the warmth of her body against his. When she had told him about Marjorie's visit, his first thought had been that everything he held dear was about to blow up in his face. For a fraction of a second he feared he might have lost Jean for good and the concept sent a cold shiver of fear through him.

He breathed another sigh of relief and settled back into the pillow. There were no more obstacles now. Nothing stood in their way. He would finish his work assignment, then…then what? He would return to Chicago? He would ask her to give up her job and go with him on blind faith without a commitment? He would stay in Seattle and turn the small public relations firm he recently purchased into his new corporate headquarters? It would be easy to do, but would it be practical? Suddenly things weren't so clear-cut anymore. He continued to hold her, but the thoughts circulating through his mind had turned from relief to disturbing.

He wanted to stop the disconcerting thoughts and concentrate on more immediate things, things that didn't leave him confused and fearful. He glanced at the clock. "It's still early. Would you like to go to a movie? Something to shove away Marjorie's manipulative attempt to involve you in one of her schemes?" *And her horrifying invasion of my life?*

"Unless you really want to, I'd just as soon stay here—"

He flashed a teasing grin. "I'd just as soon stay in bed, too."

He fluffed the pillow and pulled the blanket up around their shoulders. He cupped her breast in one hand and slid his other hand seductively down her stomach. He desperately wanted to banish Marjorie from his mind.

She batted playfully at his hand as it skimmed across her inner thigh. "That's not what I meant. I should have said that I didn't want to go out anywhere."

He placed a tender kiss on her cheek. "Of course. I knew that's what you meant." He shoved her hand away and continued to tickle his fingers across her bare skin.

The rest of the evening was lost to the growing and

expanding love that existed between them, a love that Jean readily admitted to herself and embraced, but one that frightened Ry to the point where he tried to deny it. They watched television for a while and talked about things they'd always wanted to do, places they had wanted to see. It was the type of togetherness that was so comfortable it felt as if it would last a lifetime.

Then the specter of pregnancy loomed in Jean's mind again. They had resolved one problem, but there was still a huge hurdle on the horizon, one that would not be as easy to overcome. She tried to dismiss the concerns, at least for the rest of the evening. She desperately wanted everything to be okay, for the future to hold the happiness she had always dreamed of, but had eluded her so far.

Ry spent the night at Jean's condo. There was no use in pretending that it was an unexpected happening. He had packed an overnight bag, including a change of clothes. He retrieved it from the trunk of his car early Sunday morning.

When he reached the top of the stairs, he discovered Jean turning on the water in the shower. He dropped his bag on the bed, entered the bathroom and slipped his hands inside her robe as he pulled her into his embrace.

"Would you like some company?" He flashed a teasing grin. "I'd be happy to scrub your back and you could scrub mine."

His words tickled across her cheek sending a little tremor of excitement across her skin as she spoke. "I'm afraid if we did that we'd never get anything else done. It's a beautiful day. I thought we could spend it doing something spontaneous—"

"Is this spontaneous enough for you?" He captured

her mouth with a loving kiss, one that spoke volumes about his feelings.

She allowed the kiss to continue for several seconds before breaking it off. A soft chuckle accompanied her words. "That's not what I meant."

Jean took a quick shower, then dressed and made breakfast while Ry showered, shaved and put on clean clothes. They enjoyed a quiet morning together. It felt so settled, so comfortable...so much the way she wanted things to be.

As noon approached Ry suddenly jumped to his feet, grabbed her hand and pulled her up from the sofa.

"Come on...we're going to be spontaneous."

A startled Jean looked questioningly at him, but he only grinned without divulging what he had in mind.

It turned out to be a fun and carefree afternoon. They were two people in love who, to all outward appearances, didn't have a worry in the world. They spent a delightful couple of hours browsing through Pike's Market, then they went to the aquarium. Ry had even insisted that they take the harbor cruise as if they were tourists exploring Seattle for the first time. Jean took a deep breath and slowly expelled it as the utter contentment settled over her. It had been a perfect day.

Ry stayed at Jean's condo late into the evening. They sat in front of the fireplace silently watching the flames, each comfortable and content to just be in the other's arms. He didn't want to leave her. He didn't want to go back to his hotel suite and the empty bed. He knew it wasn't a matter of sex for the sake of physical release. It was so much more, so much deeper and real. It was a physical relationship that enhanced an all consuming emotional attachment. She was all important to him— the most important thing in his life. But would he ever be able to tell her? It was a question he didn't have an answer for. A question he was afraid to answer.

Ry shifted his position, stirring Jean out of her lazy contentment. "I hate to do this, but I'm afraid I have to head back to my hotel room. It's late and tomorrow is the start of the work week." He kissed her tenderly on the forehead, then on the cheek. "It's been a lovely weekend, at least the Saturday night and Sunday part of it. Thank you for spending it with me."

"I really enjoyed our impromptu adventure today. It's been a long time since I've been that spontaneous."

He rose to his feet, then pulled her into his arms. "I hope we can spend a lot more days like this." He lingered a few minutes longer, not wanting to leave her company. Finally he kissed her tenderly on the lips, picked up his overnight bag and reluctantly left.

Jean watched as he backed his car out of her driveway and drove down the street. Sunday had been such a glorious day. It had almost erased from her mind that terrible moment when she had opened the door to Marjorie—a moment that brought back the shame and guilt from her past, the unbearable moment when she found out she had been played for a fool and used by a man she trusted. Would Ry ever be able to understand how something like that could happen? How someone could be so totally manipulated by someone else's selfish demands? Would it be part of her past that she would ever be able to share with him? She didn't know.

But before that obstacle could be tackled there was a much more important and imminent situation to deal with. There was the fact that she was pregnant with Ry's child and somehow he needed to be told. Would it mean the end of their relationship? A cold shudder confirmed a possibility she didn't want to acknowledge.

Eight

Ry spent most of the work week with the shipping and receiving department, the stockroom and the purchasing department, as all three areas were tightly interrelated. Jean saw very little of him during the day. She tried to concentrate on her own work, but each passing day her thoughts were more and more consumed by what she knew was her pregnancy, even though she still held out a desperate hope that it wasn't true.

But her nights were a different story. Each night she would be enveloped in the glow of love as she and Ry spent the evening together, sometimes with him staying all night and sometimes with him returning to his hotel suite early enough to be able to do some work before going to bed.

By Friday Jean was hardly able to keep her anxiety under control when she was around Ry. Fear had kept her from reconfirming her pregnancy with another round of home test kits. Intellectually she knew that putting off taking the home tests and going to the doctor would not change the outcome, but emotionally she made a desperate grasp for anything that would postpone the inevitable.

Before he left Jarvis Furniture for the day, Ry stopped by her office for a quick conversation.

He closed the door and perched on the edge of her desk, taking her hand in his as if he were unable to resist the temptation to touch her. "I have a lot of work to do, so if you don't mind I think I'll go directly to my hotel room and lock myself in tonight."

She hesitated a moment before asking the question, well aware of the way he had refused to discuss the work project with her. "Are there problems?"

"No...it's just that I haven't spent much of my evening time doing the work the assignment requires." A sheepish grin tugged at the corners of his mouth. "I've been far too busy enjoying much more pleasurable pursuits with a delightful companion and now I have to pay for allowing the distraction."

A quick flush spread across her cheeks. "Oh? I didn't realize I was such a distraction."

He placed a quick kiss on her lips. "Well, you are. However, I want you to be ready tomorrow morning with an overnight bag packed because I have planned a spontaneous weekend for us out of town."

She returned a teasing smile. "How can it be spontaneous if you've planned it?"

He winked at her as he squeezed her hand. "It's spontaneous for you, not for me. I've enjoyed planning it and I hope you enjoy doing it. I'll see you at five o'clock tomorrow morning."

"Five o'clock?" Her eyes widened in surprise. "Why so early?"

"Because it will take us a while to get where we're going." He brushed a quick kiss across her lips and flashed a teasing grin. "And that's all the information you're going to get out of me."

A few minutes later Ry left her office. She was disappointed that she would not be seeing him that night, but there was also a sensation of relief attached to it. It would give her an evening to try to get her head together and figure out what she needed to do.

She stopped at the drugstore on her way home from work. That evening she took three more pregnancy tests. The last of her desperate hopes were dashed by the results. A sinking sensation settled inside her like a hard lump. All three tests said the same thing, confirming the earlier tests she had taken. She was pregnant. The instructions on the box claimed a ninety-nine percent accuracy, the same as the other tests.

Her mind raced for some sort of reassurance that everything would be all right in spite of the test results. After all, there was still that one percent chance that all six of the tests were flawed. She heaved a deep sigh of resignation. In her heart she knew she was reaching for a glimmer that didn't exist. She had to stop lying to herself, stop trying to convince herself that it wasn't so. She had to face up to the reality. A cold shiver darted across the surface of her skin, sending a chill up her spine.

And she had to find the right words to tell Ry.

Her thoughts turned to what Ry had arranged for the weekend, a special weekend out of town. He intended it to be a time of pleasure and togetherness for just the two of them, not a confrontation or an airing of awkward problems. She made her decision. She would not tell him right away. She would not put a damper on their weekend.

Somewhere in the back of her mind she knew she was still grasping at straws, using any excuse to postpone the inevitable. She tried to dismiss the thought as being ridiculous, but she wasn't able to. A chilling fear washed through her, leaving only uncertainty and bewilderment in its wake.

Ry had two more weeks on his contracted assignment at Jarvis Custom Furniture. He had not mentioned any plans beyond that. Would he be staying in town or immediately returning home to get on with his life? She had to tell him before then. She had to let him know before it was time for him to leave Seattle. She had two weeks yet. She tried to gather her determination and put a positive face on things. During that time she would find the right words to tell him.

She allowed her mind to drift to how much easier it would be if only she knew what his true feelings were toward her. Did he love her or was this only a short-term fling, as Marjorie had stated? If he loved her, why hadn't he said so? Could he possibly love her as much as she loved him?

A sob caught in her throat as the mist of tears clouded her eyes. What should be the happiest time of her life—a man she loved and a baby on the way to complete the family she had always wanted—was becoming a quagmire of fears and doubts and she didn't know what to do about it. She took a steadying breath. She couldn't allow her inner turmoil to spoil the weekend Ry had planned. Somehow by tomorrow morning she needed to get her emotions corralled and present a happy and contented persona for the weekend.

She forced an upbeat attitude as she took care of some household chores, then fixed herself some dinner. She turned her attention to packing an overnight bag to take with her in the morning. Even though she tried to keep positive thoughts, her mind kept returning to the results of the pregnancy tests.

As she prepared for bed a single tear slowly etched its way down her cheek, then another and another. She wiped them away as she climbed under the covers, then reached over and turned out the lamp on the nightstand. She forced her mind to pleasant thoughts before falling asleep. She didn't want dreams filled with turmoil. But despite her attempts, her dreams weren't all happy ones. There was the always present specter of confronting Ry about her pregnancy.

She woke at four o'clock, an hour before Ry's scheduled arrival. She took her time in the shower, dressed and checked her overnight bag to make sure she hadn't forgotten anything. Then promptly at five o'clock Ry rang the doorbell.

He pulled her into his arms, kissed her, then grabbed her bag and escorted her out to his car. Jean looked up at the dark night sky as she settled in the passenger side. "It looks like the middle of the night rather than five o'clock in the morning. Aren't you going to tell me where we're going?"

Ry grinned at Jean as he slid in behind the steering wheel. "Nope...you'll find out soon enough."

"But I don't know if I packed the appropriate clothes."

"Don't worry. If there's anything you need while we're gone, I'll buy it for you."

Ry headed the car north out of Seattle. By six-thirty they had arrived at the town of Anacortes. He drove to the Washington State Ferry terminal, paid for a car, driver and passenger and pulled his car into the designated boarding lane. He turned in the seat until he faced her.

"So…any questions you'd like to ask about our destination?"

"Well, since you paid for passage to Orcas Island I'll assume that's where we're going. Right?"

He grinned, then leaned over and placed a tender kiss on her lips. "You win first prize." His expression turned serious, his voice became soft and his manner loving. He cupped her chin in his hand. "I've made reservations at a unique little bed and breakfast, no telephone and no interruptions. A romantic weekend for just the two of us."

His touch sent little tremors of delight rushing through her body and his words chased them with waves of excitement. She returned his smile. "It sounds delightful."

"But for right now—" he glanced at his watch "—we have about an hour before the next ferry to Orcas Island. Let's go into the terminal and get some hot coffee. We'll be able to get something to eat after we board the ferry."

They walked hand in hand to the terminal building. It was the start of what Jean knew would be a marvelous weekend with the most wonderful and sexy man in the world. He had chosen a romantic getaway and planned the entire weekend just for the two of them. Maybe…just maybe, if the time and circumstances were right, she would be able to tell him about the pregnancy before they returned to the reality of daily life.

It turned out to be a glorious two days filled with carefree romance and the joy of shared intimate moments. They took long walks during the day, browsed through shops filled with the work of local artisans, enjoyed the beautiful scenery and made love with a heated passion as if no one else in the world even existed.

Their weekend came to a close Sunday night as they reluctantly boarded the ferry to return to Anacortes. It had been an idyllic getaway, a time she had chosen to not spoil by introducing the subject of pregnancy. She convinced herself that it was a topic better left to another time and place, perhaps a quiet moment set aside specifically for that purpose rather than trying to incorporate it with another activity. The reality of how wrong that notion was tried to override her conscious decision, but she refused to allow it. She would handle it, but at another time, rather than now. The nervous anxiety churning inside her only confirmed how absurd she knew that decision was.

Neither of them said much on the drive from Anacortes back to Seattle. Each basked in the warm glow of the love that surrounded them. It was after eleven o'clock Sunday night when Ry pulled into the driveway of Jean's condo. He carried her overnight bag as they walked to the front door. As soon as they were inside, he dropped the bag to the floor and pulled her into his embrace.

"Thank you for the enchanting weekend, Ry. It was marvelous."

His words tickled across her cheek. "Thank you for sharing it with me. My only regret is that it was so short."

He lowered his head and placed a tender and loving kiss on her lips—a kiss that was as much emotion as passion, a kiss that told how much he cared about her. A kiss that said what he had not been able to convey in words. It was a truth he could no longer deny. He was totally in love with Jean Summerfield. He had finally admitted it to himself, but didn't know what to say or how to say it to her. His work assignment would be over in two weeks. By that time he had to have made a decision. Stay or go...ask her to go with him...try to maintain a long distance relationship.

He didn't know what to do, but he did know that it would probably give him more than one restless night before he worked up the courage to do what he knew in his heart had to be done. He had to make a commitment to her, but what kind of commitment? A commitment to a relationship? Possibly even marriage?

The notion of marriage shocked him. It was the last thing he would have consciously considered, yet the thought was there as crystal clear as the other thoughts running through his mind. But what to do about it? He didn't know and time was running out. He couldn't allow the way Marjorie had manipulated him into marriage by claiming to be pregnant to affect his relationship with Jean. He knew Jean was so honest and real, that she would never be guilty of the same type of subterfuge that was common to Marjorie's everyday life.

"I'd better head back to the hotel and get some sleep. For most of the upcoming week I'll be spending my time in the manufacturing plant with the various operations there, so I probably won't see much of you during the day. I'll be covering all the office functions during the final week."

They talked for a few more minutes, then Ry placed a gentle kiss on her lips before he left. He seemed to be bouncing on a cloud of euphoria as he walked to his car, his head filled with happy and contented thoughts. How lucky he had been to have found Sally Jean again. She was so honest, so sincere...just as she had been in high school. He had business associates, employees and even a few friends whom he trusted, but it had been a long time since he felt an emotional trust with anyone on an intimate level. Jean had turned out to be that person. She was truly genuine, someone he knew he could trust with anything…including the vulnerability he had kept so carefully hidden away for the past ten years.

Once again Jean watched him drive away. She closed her eyes and allowed her thoughts to drift over the weekend they had just spent together.

She had come very close to telling him about being pregnant, but the time never seemed absolutely right. She had been looking for the perfect moment even though she knew no such thing as an ideal time existed to disclose the type of news she had. She felt relief that she hadn't been subjected to the confrontation, yet at the same time an uneasiness about not having told him. She couldn't put it off much longer. She knew she had to tell him before the upcoming week was over. But how?

A sudden and deep sorrow tried to force itself on her. What if he didn't really love her, at least not enough to build a future? What if he didn't want the baby? What if he didn't want her when he found out she was pregnant? The sorrow tried to turn into a sob, followed by tears welling in her eyes. She blinked them away. There was no question that she was handling the situation badly. She had to tell him. She had to find a way. The tears slowly trickled down her cheeks. How could she be so much in love yet so miserable all at the same time?

Jean unpacked her overnight bag and prepared for bed. She fell asleep quickly, but it was not a peaceful night. Rather than the euphoria of the weekend providing pleasant dreams, she tossed and turned as her mind filled with everything that could go wrong when she told Ry about her pregnancy.

She continued with an unsettled night, finally waking half an hour before the alarm went off.

The morning started the beginning of another work week. Ry had been correct, she saw very little of him during the days that followed. He had also reluctantly been absent from her life for most evenings during the week due to a heavy work load that he had been neglecting while he had spent almost every night with her. She barely saw him for more than a few minutes at a time until Wednesday night.

The tension had been building inside her all day and now it was almost six o'clock. Ry was due to pick her up any minute to take her out to dinner. Her tattered nerves told her just how high her stress level had risen. Her life seemed to be torn into two facets. One part loved Ry more than anything, reveled in the days and hours they had to themselves and wanted them to last forever. The other part knew telling him could not be put off any longer, regardless of how much it frightened her or how it would impact the future.

As soon as he arrived at her condo he immediately pulled her into his arms and captured her mouth with a kiss that spoke of pent-up desires, incendiary passion and a deep and abiding love. And everything else faded from her mind.

"I've really missed you. This has been worse than when I was in Chicago for a couple of days. At least there was a good reason for my not being able to see you then. We were two thousand miles apart. But this week has been impossible. You don't know how often I wanted to go to your office and close the door, but I needed to stay with the manufacturing operation. And the nights…" He stroked her hair as he nestled her head against his shoulder. "There were so many times I wanted to shove the work aside and drive over here just so I could see your face, touch your cheek and taste your lips.''

He continued to hold her, not wanting to relinquish the warm sensation. ''You are such an enchanting temptress that I haven't been able to stay away from you. It's almost as if you'd cast some kind of a spell over me that I couldn't fight.''

''Stop it.'' A soft chuckle escaped her throat as the heat flushed across her cheeks. ''You're embarrassing me.''

''It's the simple truth.'' He placed a tender kiss on her forehead. ''And as a result, I've allowed my work requirements to fall far behind schedule and now I'm forced to play catch up. I need to have all the reports completed by Thursday of next week so I can submit them to Matt the next day. So, if I'm going to have this weekend free for us, I'm afraid I need to work at night. This was the only evening I could get some extra time.''

He lifted her chin so he could look into her eyes. ''I hope you understand.''

''Of course I do. After all, you have a contracted assignment and it needs to be finished on schedule.''

''So…I've made reservations for us for dinner tonight. Are you ready?'' He was reluctant to turn loose of her, but they needed to be on their way. And if they didn't leave right then he knew the next step would be up the stairs to her bedroom—certainly a very appealing and desirable alternative.

''Yes, and I'm hungry.''

They went to dinner at a charming, out of the way restaurant where they enjoyed a delicious meal enveloped in the aura of love that surrounded them. They lingered with after-dinner coffee. She was so thrilled to be with Ry again. She didn't want anything to spoil the perfect evening. Following dinner they returned to her condo.

Would this be the proper time to tell Ry? The last three days since they had returned from Orcas Island had been filled with longings and fears. The trembling started again, the deep tremors that assaulted her insides and said her anxiety level had reached a new high.

She had planned to tell him as soon as he arrived, but decided it would be better to wait until they returned from dinner. They had left her condo too quickly and the restaurant was obviously not the proper setting. Should she do it now? Wait for a little while and tell him later that evening? It was already getting late. Maybe it would be better to tell him this weekend when she wouldn't feel as rushed, when they would have time to discuss the ramifications.

Yes, that would be better. The decision lessened her immediate trepidation, but did nothing to calm her nerves. The evening had been so perfect. She didn't want to destroy the mood and atmosphere by bringing up what she knew was going to be a difficult subject, especially when it was too late that evening to devote much time to it.

She also knew she was only fooling herself by putting it off. Was she living in a dream world? Hoping for some kind of miracle that would somehow make everything all right? She told herself no, but she didn't believe it.

Ry spent the night with her, a night containing all the passion and love they had shared over the weekend on Orcas Island. A blissfully happy Jean snuggled into his embrace under the covers. It had only been a few days, but she had missed him so much—missed the warmth of his touch, the passion of his kiss, the earthiness of his sensuality. She also missed talking to him, sharing dreams and ideas with him. Life with Ry would be so perfect. Then she again recalled the task ahead of her. The turmoil played havoc with her senses. She fell asleep in his arms, but an uneasiness continued to circulate through her mind as she slept.

Ry woke early the next morning so he could return to his hotel and prepare for another day at work. He paused at the front door and pulled Jean into his arms. "I'm afraid the rest of this week will be pretty much like the first part. I'll be lucky to catch a glimpse of you at work and I'll be working tonight and tomorrow night at the hotel."

He placed a soft kiss on her lips. "Let's do something Saturday... I don't care what as long as we do it together. You plan the day for us, whatever you want to do."

He squeezed her hand, then turned loose of her. "I'll call you tonight."

She watched as he left. She had allowed yet another opportunity to slip away without telling Ry she was pregnant. She couldn't let it happen again. First thing Saturday morning, as soon as he arrived to pick her up, she would tell him. The churning trepidation told her just how much she feared the outcome, but she didn't know why. If Ry loved her, then everything should be all right. But did he love her? He had never said and not knowing preyed on her mind more and more with each passing day.

She rallied her determination. Saturday morning would be it. There wouldn't be any more postponements or excuses.

Ry stepped out of the shower and towel dried his hair. The work week was finished and he had caught up on a lot of the backlog by working nights for the past week. In less than an hour he would be with Jean again for the weekend. A strange combination of elation and anxiety twisted around inside him.

He didn't like the unsettled nature of his relationship with her. He wasn't happy not knowing what the future held. It had taken a lot of internal battle, but he had finally made his decision before going to bed last night. And now after sleeping on that decision, it still felt right. In fact, nothing had ever felt more right.

He planned to put everything on the line—his emotions, his heart, his carefully buried vulnerability. He would tell her he loved her and offer her a commitment. He didn't know yet what the details of that commitment would be or how they would work out their careers, but he knew they would be able to do it. The important thing was that they would be together…forever. And if that meant marriage, then that was what it would be.

He finished dressing, grabbed his jacket and drove to Jean's. It was still early, not even eight o'clock yet. He would take her out to breakfast, maybe to the restaurant at the top of the Space Needle so they could enjoy the spectacular view as the restaurant revolved.

The joy of his decision to offer Jean a commitment continued to well inside him as he approached her front door. To his surprise, the door flung open as soon as he stepped on the porch.

He immediately pulled her into his arms and kissed her, the moment even more special because of his decision. He couldn't hold back the grin that played at the corners of his mouth. "I have something I want to discuss with you. I planned to do it before I took you out to breakfast and we started on whatever adventure you had planned for the day, but judging by the way you opened the door you must really be hungry. Maybe we should go to breakfast first.''

She nervously shifted her weight as she took a step back from his embrace. She had to escape the mesmerizing pull of his touch. She needed to keep her head clear and her emotions in tight control. ''I've…uh…I've been waiting for you.''

Her nervousness immediately telegraphed to him. Something was wrong. ''Jean? Is there a problem?'' A tickle of panic tried to take hold. A sense of urgency surrounded his words. ''Are you okay?''

''It's…we have to talk. I have something I need to tell you and it can't be put off any longer.''

''Of course.'' He forced a calm outer manner, but it didn't prevent his insides from twisting into a thousand knots. Somewhere in the back of his mind a tiny spark of fear tried to ignite into a conscious thought. What if she was sick? If she had been diagnosed with some sort of life threatening disease? He pulled together his determination and shoved down his fears. Whatever it was he would take care of her. He would see to it that she got well again. A cold shudder rippled through his body. The thought of anything happening to her was almost more than he could handle.

He took a calming breath. He was letting his imagination run wild. He needed to get back to reality. She couldn't be sick. It had to be something else. Maybe a financial problem of some sort. He knew he was grasping at straws. He took her hand and led her to the sofa.

''Sit down and tell me what the problem is. Whatever it is that's bothering you—'' he paused a moment to recapture his rapidly deteriorating composure ''—we can work it out together.'' He had to be strong so he could give her the strength and emotional support she obviously needed.

Jean looked up at him. He looked so concerned, a deep concern that touched her heart. Maybe all of her anxieties and worries had been for no reason. The tension began to ease out of her body. She closed her eyes and drew in a steadying breath. The best thing to do was just say it outright without beating around the bush. She took in another deep breath, held it a few seconds, then slowly exhaled. She reached out and took his hand. She desperately needed the warmth and comfort of his touch and the strength he personified.

"Ry…" She gulped down the lump in her throat and tried to control the quaver in her voice. She finally forced out the words that had so frightened her. "I…I'm pregnant."

She saw the shock spread across his face and felt his muscles tense before he let go of her hand. He jumped to his feet. The concern that had been in his eyes disappeared, to be replaced for an instant by a stormy confusion before turning angry. A sick churning boiled up from the pit of her stomach. Any hope she had for him being pleased with her news, or at the very least readily accepting it, had been dashed.

"Ry?" Her voice filled with the fear that coursed through her veins. "Say something…please."

He finally forced out some words. "You're…you're pregnant?" His voice grew angrier, his words accusatory. "How can that be? I always take precautions."

"Not that first time…not after all the champagne we had at the rehearsal dinner."

The words came out even before he thought about them. "So that's your claim?" He heard the hard edge to his voice and wasn't sure exactly where it had come from. "The first time we made love you got pregnant because we had too much to drink?"

The pain sliced through him like a hot knife through butter. It swirled around inside him, mixing with the sudden anger until he couldn't tell them apart. Everything he believed in and held true had been pulled out from under him in the blink of an eye. He loved Jean and more importantly, he had trusted her. And now she was saying almost the exact same words Marjorie had uttered so convincingly ten years ago, the deception and manipulation she had used to trap him into marrying her.

Was that Jean's game, too? If she had waited a little while longer she wouldn't have had to use the lie. He would have asked her to marry him because he loved her. But now…he shook his head hoping it would clear out the bad dream and the horrible pain. Only it wasn't a dream. Everything he wanted, everything he believed in came crashing down around him.

Every self-protective instinct he had ever possessed, every defense mechanism he had developed from childhood on through adulthood suddenly kicked into play. He had allowed his vulnerability to come out of its safe hiding place and now he was paying the price. He staggered backward a couple of steps as he desperately fought to maintain control of his spiraling panic. The words seemed to come out of his mouth before he could even formulate the thoughts.

"What's the name of your doctor?"

"My doctor?"

He saw the hurt and confusion on her face, but refused to let it penetrate the protective wall he had put between them, a wall built from bricks made of old wounds and ancient hurts. He had to look away in order to steel himself against his own emotions and the love he felt for her, a love he knew deep in his heart would never go away.

"Yes…your doctor. The one who confirmed your pregnancy."

"I…I haven't been to the doctor yet. I have an appointment for week after next."

"Then how do you know you're pregnant?"

"I took a home pregnancy—"

"And on the basis of something you claim to have bought over the counter at the drugstore you now expect me to…to do what?"

He closed his eyes as he tried to regain his composure. He had hoped she would be able to give him a name, be able to say she had been to the doctor and the pregnancy was confirmed. But again her words echoed those Marjorie had said to him ten years ago—a home pregnancy test. Well, he had been down that road before and he didn't want to take that painful journey again. He knew he needed to get away from her physical presence, to leave before his love overruled the reality of what she was trying to do to him.

"I won't be manipulated this way…not again. If you get this confirmed by a doctor, let me know."

His voice was cold, his physical manner distant. She fought back the tears that threatened to·flood down her cheeks. The last thing she wanted was for him to see her cry. He would probably think it was nothing more than another attempt to manipulate him, to use his own word. The horrible pain and the heavy weight of betrayal settled over her. Nothing in her life had been as unbearable as the total and complete rejection she had just experienced. She tried to pull herself together, at least long enough to get him out her door.

"No." She saw the surprise dart across his features.

"No? What do you mean by no?"

"Just what I said. No—I won't be bothering you with a doctor's report." She heard the bitterness and pain that came out in her voice, but she didn't care. "You may consider your responsibility in this matter finished as of this moment. I certainly don't want you to feel as if you were being manipulated in any way."

Jean walked to the front door, opened it and stood aside clearly indicating that she wanted him to leave.

Ry hesitated for a moment, not sure what to do. His mind swirled in a mass of confusion. She was throwing him out? Dismissing him? He had steeled himself against a totally different type of reaction from her. He had been prepared for her to attempt to coerce him into staying, not for her to tell him to leave. Had he been too hasty in his decision? Had he been wrong to assume—

"Goodbye, Ryland."

Her words cut into his thoughts and penetrated his hurt and anger. They sounded so final. He looked at her, but she refused to make eye contact with him. She looked so determined, so sure of her decision. Doubts flooded through him battering his sense of reality against the rocks. Had he made a colossal blunder?

"Wait a minute. Perhaps—"

"I said goodbye, Ryland. I want you to leave right now."

Her tone of voice left him no room for argument or discussion. He turned and walked out the door and as he did every fiber of his existence started to unravel. It felt as if his life had just come unglued. He started to turn back, but heard the door slam with a finality that left nothing to the imagination. Then the sounds of uncontrollable sobbing reached his ears. It tore out what little was left of his composure.

He sat in his car for what seemed like forever before he finally came out of his stupor enough to start the engine. His senses were numb, but not enough to prevent him from choking on the emotions and pain that were pulling him apart.

He hadn't allowed himself to cry since that horrible Christmas when he was eight years old and his beloved train had been taken away from him. That was twenty-four years ago. But right now he felt like that eight-year-old boy again and he wanted to drown his sorrow with tears, only he wasn't eight years old anymore. He was an adult who was totally in love and had just made what was probably the most colossal mistake of his life.

Nine

Jean looked at the clock for what seemed like the hundredth time since the alarm had gone off half an hour ago. It was almost seven o'clock. She had spent the most miserable weekend of her life. Following Ry's stormy departure Saturday morning until she went to bed Sunday night, she had moved almost trancelike from the chair to the sofa to the floor to the bed and back to the chair again. She knew she hadn't gotten more than six or seven hours sleep total for both Saturday night and Sunday night. The loneliness pulled at her, reinforcing her feelings of abandonment by everyone and everything she loved and held dear.

Each time she was sure she had finally cried out every last tear in her body, the whole thing would start all over again. She had never known that much pain, never believed anything could be as horrific as Ry's immediate and total rejection. It couldn't have hurt more if he had doubled up his fist and landed a solid punch.

Never in her wildest flights of imagination would she ever have guessed that this would be Ry's reaction to her being pregnant. It was so sudden, so swift, so painful…and felt so final. One moment he was caring and tender and the next he was angry and accusing her of trying to manipulate him. It was as if he had turned into a totally different person. She closed her eyes as the tears tried to overflow the brims again. She loved him so much. How could this have happened?

She tried once again to get her emotions under control. She had to get out of bed. It was Monday morning and she needed to be at work in an hour. She would have to hurry if she was going to be on time and being on time was absolutely mandatory. This was the week Ry would be evaluating the various office procedures and that included her personnel department. The last thing she wanted to do was give him an excuse to put something negative into his report.

His report—a shudder of fear made its way through her body. She was pregnant and alone. She had no one to depend on other than herself. She needed her job now more than ever. Would he try to get back at her by giving her a bad report? Surely he wouldn't do such a mean, vindictive thing. But she knew it was up to her to make sure he had no reason to.

Reluctantly she climbed out of bed and headed for the shower. She moved mechanically through the process of putting on her makeup, dressing and leaving for work. She arrived five minutes before eight o'clock, taking note of the fact that Ry's car was already in his parking space. The anxiety knotted in the pit of her stomach as she entered the building. What should she say to him?

Should she speak first or only acknowledge him if he made a direct comment to her? How should she act in front of the man she loved with all her heart—the man who had so easily dismissed her from his life?

The tears welled in her eyes again. She glanced around, hoping that no one would notice. She saw Ry headed in her direction. She turned away and hurried to the rest room. The last thing she wanted was for Ry to know how much he had hurt her. She reached the rest room door just as he approached her office, managing to duck inside before he could stop her.

Jean splashed some cold water on her eyes in an attempt to keep them from looking red and puffy. She had to get through five days of contact with Ry Collier. Five days in which her life would be in constant turmoil wondering what he was going to put into his report. Five days of seeing the rejection in his eyes. The sorrow once again washed over her.

And she would have a lifetime to live with the pain.

She squared her shoulders and set her determination. She certainly couldn't hide in the rest room all day. She had a job to do and responsibilities to take care of. She ran a comb through her hair, touched up her makeup around her eyes, then went to her office to start her workday.

Half an hour later, Ry entered the personnel department which consisted of a large room with half the space divided into individual cubicles for the staff and the other half filled with file cabinets and open work space. At the back of the room was one separate office for Jean where she could have her office door open to observe the workings of her department or closed if she was having a private meeting with one of the company employees.

He walked casually through the outer office, pausing

to say a polite good morning to everyone before arriving at Jean's office door.

"Do you have a moment, Jean?"

"Yes, Mr. Collier. Of course." She set aside the file folder and exited the computer program she had been working with, then looked up at him. "What can I do for you?"

Her manner was formal and her voice cold, but the worst of it was the pain he glimpsed in her eyes before she shifted her gaze away from him. He knew this initial meeting with her following their explosive encounter on Saturday morning wasn't going to be easy. He had been giving it a lot of thought over the weekend. A lot of thought…that was a laugh. He hadn't thought of anything else. He also hadn't eaten and had barely managed a few hours of restless sleep. In short, he had been miserable and he knew it was his own doing.

Rather than responding to what she had said on its own merits, he had reacted based on all the stored resentment he harbored against Marjorie. It had been wrong. Jean was not Marjorie. Jean was the woman he loved and she deserved much better than she got. He had hurt her deeply and somehow he had to make it right.

He sat on the edge of her desk. "Jean…we need to talk."

"I believe you said all there was to say Saturday morning. So, if that's all you want you'll have to excuse me. I have a very busy schedule today and can't afford any wasted time."

He knew this was going to be difficult and the office certainly wasn't the place to do it, but he desperately needed to clear the air between them so he could at least lay the foundation for them to discuss things that evening.

"Give me a break here, Jean. I'm trying—"

Her volume increased with her anger. Her eyes widened in shock. "Give you a break?"

She glanced toward her office door, noting that a couple of the staff members seemed to have been attracted by her comments. She rose from her chair and walked around her desk until her back was to the outer office, but didn't want to confirm any suspicions her staff might have had by closing the door.

She lowered her voice. "This is a business office, Mr. Collier. What we conduct here is company business. I would appreciate it if you would confine your conversation to that and that alone."

He rose to his feet. "Certainly, business it shall be. I want to see the employee manual you hand out when someone is hired and I want to see the job descriptions you have on file for the various departments and positions within those departments."

His rapid change in manner threw her for a loop, but not as much as the type of information he was asking for. "Uh…well…yes, we do have an employee informational sheet that we hand out." She reached into her desk and pulled out a file. She took out a sheet of paper and handed it to him.

He took it from her, glanced at the front side, then turned it over and looked at the back. He leveled a questioning gaze at her as he held up the piece of paper. "This is it? You don't have any type of employee manual?"

She spit out the words between clenched teeth. "That's it."

"What about the job descriptions?"

"That's usually handled by the department head where the person is going to work."

"You don't have something already in print? Some sort of a job description for the people working in your department?"

"Uh...no." She felt her hackles rise. Was she hearing yet more accusation in his voice? Disapproval? She clipped her words as she spoke, her anger barely held beneath the surface. "I've never had the need to put one together."

"I see. Do you think you could have something for me by the end of the day?"

"I have several other things that need to be done today, but I'll certainly try."

"Good."

She watched as his gaze swept around her office, lingering on file cabinets and the numerous in and out baskets, then peering out her door to the large outer office with its cubicles and furniture arrangement. Without warning he slid off the edge of her desk, turned and walked out of her office.

Jean went about her normal daily routine, as much as she could. It seemed that every time she looked up she saw Ry either watching her, watching her employees or asking them questions. And each time it sent a tremor of anxiety through her body. She made a special effort to provide him with the information he had asked for, but when she gave it to him the only response was a polite thank-you as he put it in his attaché case without looking at it.

She had never been so thankful to see the end of a workday as she was when five o'clock arrived. She quickly gathered her things and rushed toward her car, wanting to make her escape before she encountered Ry again. Fortunately she had a meeting with her little theater group that night which saved her from having nothing to do other than go home. She stopped at the grocery store on her way home after the meeting. By the time she put the few groceries away, it was after eleven o'clock and she was tired.

As soon as she entered her bedroom she saw the red message light flashing on her answering machine. There were four messages. The muscles in her stomach instantly tightened. She reached for the button to play back the messages.

"Jean...it's Ry. If you're there, please pick up the phone...Jean? Are you there? We have to talk. I must...uh...I want to apologize...the way I acted Saturday morning...it's...well, what you said was such a shock...uh, Jean...we have to talk. Please call me as soon as you get in. We have to talk."

She stopped the playback of the messages. He sounded so unsure of himself, so hesitant. It was something that she would never have associated with Ry Collier. She didn't know what to do. He sounded so sincere in his desire for them to talk, but was it only to smooth over the way he had handled the situation? Would he really have anything different to say? He had made it so clear that he refused to accept the pregnancy and that they were through. What could he possibly have to say that would change the situation?

The heavy weight of despair settled over her. Why couldn't he just leave it alone? Was he trying to vacuum his conscience? Somehow she would manage to muddle through four more days of work, then he would be gone and she would be able to put the shattered pieces of her life back together. She played the remaining messages, all three of them from Ry.

She erased the messages, then prepared for bed. Suddenly she was very tired and emotionally exhausted. All she wanted to do was sleep. Perhaps when she woke up she would find that all of this had been a horrible nightmare.

When Jean arrived at work Tuesday morning, she spotted Ry in the accounting department. She hurried to her office. Hopefully he would spend the day with the accounting people and leave her department alone. She was still stinging from his attitude about an employee manual and job descriptions. Although, in retrospect, she had to grudgingly admit that he had been correct. It was something she should have done a long time ago rather than trying to make do with the meager information she handed out.

It's just that she was so busy with the myriad of miscellaneous tasks that continually landed on her desk. She didn't have time to truly reorganize things the way they should be even though she knew it would be more efficient. Was it something that he would hold against her when he did his report? A nervous anxiety jittered inside her. It would be a derogatory comment she couldn't refute.

That afternoon Ry stationed himself in the outer office of the personnel department. It seemed that every time Jean looked up from her desk Ry would be snooping in files or talking to her staff members. With each passing hour her nerves stretched thinner and thinner until she thought they would break. Five o'clock finally arrived. She cleaned the top of her desk and prepared to leave, but before she could get out her office door, Ry blocked her way.

"I called you several times last night and left messages for you to call me, but you never returned my calls."

She made it a point to be civil, but there was no reason to be anything less than formal. "It was very late when I got your messages. I was tired and went right to bed."

"It's not late now. We can go to your place and talk this out."

"I don't see why there's anything left to say. As I told you yesterday, you made your position very clear Saturday morning. I'm sure you have many more important things to do than going over old ground with me, especially when it won't change the fact that I'm pregnant. I've already told you that I won't hold you to any responsibility in this matter, either emotional or financial. You have no obligation to me or the baby."

She quickly swallowed to prevent the sob from creeping into her voice. "I am fully capable of taking care of myself. That leaves us with nothing to discuss. Now—" she picked up her purse and car keys "—I'm finished here for the day and want to leave."

She quickly brushed by him before he had an opportunity to say anything. It had taken every bit of her internal fortitude to remain calm while talking to him. The tremors of apprehension tried to make their way down her legs, threatening to turn them to rubber. She hurried out of the building, desperate to get to her car and then home.

Two days down and three to go before Ry would be finished at Jarvis Custom Furniture and out of her daily life. Maybe then she could start to put the shattered pieces back together. And what about his final report? Would it have an adverse effect on her job? A cold shiver darted up her spine telling her just how fearful she was of the prospect of raising a child alone while needing to work full-time to support herself and that child. Nothing had ever frightened her as much as that did. She had to be strong. She needed to rally more internal strength than ever before in her life. The tears tried to form in her eyes, but she quickly brushed them away.

Wednesday and Thursday came and went with Jean doing her best to avoid Ry without being obvious about it in front of her staff. To her relief he didn't call her either night and when she arrived at work Friday morning he wasn't there. When he hadn't appeared by noon, she began to breathe a little easier.

Shortly after lunch Matt Jarvis appeared in her office. "Jean, I just wanted to let you know that Ry Collier has completed his evaluation and his final reports will be available by four o'clock this afternoon. I'll be giving each department manager a copy of the portion pertaining to their specific department so the report can be studied over the weekend. On Monday morning we'll have a meeting of the department heads to discuss the reports and talk about implementing the procedures he has suggested. I'd like to start the meeting at seven o'clock. Will that early time be okay for you?"

She smiled and extended a confident manner. "Of course, Matt. I'll be there."

As soon as Matt left her office, her forced smile faded and was quickly replaced by a slight frown. What would be in his report? She glanced at the clock on her office wall. In another two hours she'd know for sure. Half an hour later she spotted Ry headed toward Matt's office with a large envelope in his hand. Her muscles tensed and a sinking sensation left her almost light-headed. This was it. She would soon know her fate and what additional changes she would need to make for the future. She drew in a calming breath in an attempt to settle the nervous tension jittering through her body.

She kept busy while also keeping one eye on the time.

A few minutes after four o'clock Matt entered her office. He handed her the report. "Here you go, Jean. Study these recommendations and we'll discuss them first thing Monday morning."

She hesitated a moment, then took the envelope from him. "Of course, Matt. I'll go over the report very carefully this weekend."

She placed the envelope on her desk, then stared at it for several minutes without opening it. The anxiety level that had been vibrating just below the surface burst into full-blown panic. She finally picked up the envelope and held it close to her body, again without opening it. Intellectually she knew it wasn't so, but somehow it seemed as if she would be spared and her job would be secure if she didn't read the report.

She finally shoved it into her purse and tried to concentrate on her work, but without much success. When five o'clock arrived she cleared her desk and left for the weekend.

Jean arrived home, changed clothes, then sat on the edge of her bed staring at the dreaded envelope. She closed her eyes and tried to calm her rampaging fears. Ignoring Ry's report wasn't going to change what he had written. Her hands trembled as she picked up the envelope and removed the contents.

She started to read. Words leaped off the page at her. *Complete overhaul of internal structure of personnel department...woefully out of date with today's business requirements...revamp interaction with other departments.* Then the most damaging words of all, words that practically screamed at her and put an immediate halt to reading the rest of the report. *Eliminate position of personnel manager.*

The pages dropped from her hands as the final stab of

betrayal sliced through her. She was pregnant, rejected by the father of her child and now he had recommended that she be fired from her job. The tears filled her eyes. How could anyone be so callous and unfeeling? He had played loose and careless with her emotions. It was a lesson she thought she had learned in the past, but this time she had learned it for good. She would never lose her heart again no matter how charming, sexy and desirable the man was.

*Eliminate position of personnel manager...*the words swirled around in her mind. It was the final blow, the ending of five weeks in her life with Ry Collier. Even though he wasn't married to Marjorie, she had apparently been right about one thing. He considered her as nothing more than a temporary out-of-town fling. And now the fling was over and he would be going back to his home in Chicago.

The sick churning in her stomach tried to make its way up her throat. She swallowed several times to tamp it back down. Then the tears broke loose and cascaded down her cheeks, the sobs convulsing through her body. She had been holding it back all day, but couldn't hold it one second longer.

The future scared her so much. She knew she had to be strong if she was going to raise a child by herself. She shook her head. This was not the way she had envisioned it would be. She had pictured a happy, loving home with Ry and their baby. And now that dream had vanished as thoroughly as if it had never existed.

The ringing doorbell startled her out of the misery. She ignored the sound. Whoever it was, she didn't want to talk to them. The persistent buzzing finally forced her into action. She descended the stairs, walked across the living room and angrily yanked open the door. She froze in her tracks when she saw Ry.

He stepped inside and closed the door without waiting to be invited. He kept his voice firm without being threatening. "I told you we need to talk, and I meant it." Then he focused on her face, the red eyes and tear streaked cheeks, and it tore at his heart. A sharp pain stabbed through him. How could he have done this to her? How could he have allowed his old demons with Marjorie to control his love for Jean and interfere with their relationship?

Somehow he had to convince her that he was not the worst bastard to ever walk the face of the earth. He pulled her into his embrace. Her body immediately stiffened, then her hands were against his chest trying to push away from him. He refused to let go.

Ry was firm in his words without being harsh. "I'm bigger than you, I'm stronger than you and I'm going to hold on to you until you calm down so you might as well stop struggling."

Several seconds passed before he felt some of the tension drain away from her body. His voice softened as he caressed her shoulders and stroked her hair. "Are you all right now? Can we sit down and talk this out?"

Her words came out as a whisper. "You don't seem to be giving me any choice in the matter."

Ry took Jean's hand and led her to the sofa, then sat next to her. He kept his arm protectively around her shoulders. An apprehensive jitter welled inside him, but he knew he had to ignore it. He had made a mess of things and it was up to him to straighten it out. No matter what the future held, he had to take care of the present before anything else.

"First of all I want to apologize to you for my deplorable behavior Saturday morning.'' A quick jab of anxiety assailed his senses and he just as quickly shoved it aside. ''I had no right to treat you that way and I feel horrible about it. I don't even have the excuse of being a confused and immature seventeen-year-old.''

He paused as he tried to get his thoughts in order. Knowing he had only one chance to redeem himself he had to carefully assess every word. He couldn't afford to misspeak or not be clear in what he was saying. He desperately needed to make her understand what had happened…and why.

''I want to tell you about something I swore I'd never talk about, something that only Bill Todd knows. It doesn't excuse my appalling reaction Saturday morning, but I hope it will help explain it.''

He took a deep breath, held it for several seconds, then slowly exhaled. He had given this a great deal of thought over the weekend. It was his job to analyze things and make appropriate decisions based on that analysis. But this was highly emotional. Analyzing and dealing with emotions was not an area where he excelled. He didn't want to reopen the old wounds, to expose yet another carefully hidden vulnerability, but he knew it had to be done. He didn't know any other way to repair the damage he had caused.

''It was a month after I had graduated from college. Marjorie and I had been dating for about three months. It was nothing serious, at least I didn't think so. In fact, I saw it as mostly sex and not much else. Then one night she hit me with the news that she was pregnant. Needless to say I was stunned. I asked her how that was possible since I had always taken all the proper precautions.

''She reminded me of a night about six weeks earlier when we'd been at a pregraduation celebration where the beer flowed and everyone had too much to drink. I had checked us into a motel just a block from the party rather than driving the fifteen miles back to her apartment after imbibing too much. She claimed that was the night she got pregnant, that neither one of us was lucid enough to even think about using a condom, let alone going out to find one. I couldn't refute her claim since I didn't really remember much of that night after we left the party.''

He paused as the painful memories once again took hold. ''Anyway, I did the honorable thing and married her even though I didn't love her. It was a couple of months later when I discovered the truth. She wasn't pregnant at all and never had been. She coyly batted her eyelashes at me and said it was the only way she could think of to get me to marry her.

''I filed for divorce the next day. Then I found out she had pulled the same scam on another guy three years earlier and had taken him for everything he was worth in the divorce settlement. I had a good attorney. We had several credible witnesses including her ex-husband. The judge tossed her out on her ear. He said she was a conniving schemer who didn't deserve one cent and even added that she had left herself open for a civil suit if I chose to file one. As for me, all I wanted was to get as far away from Marjorie and everything she stood for as I possibly could.''

Ry pulled Jean into his embrace. He desperately needed the warmth of her closeness, the contentment and settled feeling he had whenever he was with her. ''And that's what happened Saturday morning. You were trying to tell me about being pregnant, but what I heard was Marjorie lying to me, conning me and manipulating me into marrying her.'' He placed a tender kiss on her cheek.

"I had no right to do that to you. I had no right to impose my past on what you were saying. I'm so sorry, Jean."

He turned until he could look into her eyes. He cupped her face in his hands. "A few weeks ago you told me you could forgive the actions of a seventeen-year-old boy. Well, what happened Saturday morning was not the doing of an immature seventeen-year-old boy. It was my fault, a mature thirty-two-year-old man. I've given you an explanation for what happened, but I'm not making an excuse for my indefensible actions. There isn't any excuse for what I put you through." He brushed a soft kiss across her lips. "But once again I'm asking you to forgive me for something I never should have allowed to happen."

The apprehension churned inside him. His entire future was on the line. It seemed like forever before she said anything, then he realized he'd been holding his breath as he waited for her response.

Her voice conveyed the confusion roiling inside her. "I don't know, Ry." She shook her head as the frown wrinkled across her forehead. "I don't know what to say."

His explanation shocked her, then the reality of what it meant slowly soaked into her consciousness. It certainly did explain why he would have reacted to her news the way he did, but it didn't do anything to alleviate her anxiety. She still didn't know how he felt about her, if he loved her, whether he would accept the baby…if they could ever be a real family in a loving home with a future together.

And then there was the damaging report about her department with his recommendation that her job be eliminated. That would require a lot more explaining before she could even attempt to understand why he would do such a thing. She twisted out of his embrace. She forced the words, but she knew they needed to be said.

"So I forgive you for this. Now where does that leave us? Where do things stand? And none of this is going to alter the fact that I'm pregnant." She looked at him. "Where do we go from here, Ry? What comes next?"

She had thrown the situation squarely in his lap. He knew any attempt to postpone a serious discussion of their relationship would only make matters worse. He gathered his composure.

"When I arrived here last Saturday morning I said I had something I wanted to discuss with you. I wanted to discuss the future. Perhaps this would be the time for that discussion."

"What about the future?"

He pulled her into his arms again. "I believe you about being pregnant." His anxiety rose again. He was about to move into new territory, to put his last vestige of vulnerability on the line, but before he could say any more, his fear won out. He balked. He didn't say what he had wanted to. He didn't tell her he loved her.

"I want very much to be a part of your life. I want to help raise our child."

Her words were defiant. "Are you saying that because you feel obligated? If so, don't bother. I don't want you to feel that you're being pressured into something." She paused as his words about Marjorie popped into her mind. "I don't want you to resent me because you feel like you're being manipulated."

The panic rose inside him. He didn't know what to say. No, that's not true. He knew what to say—he knew he had to tell her he loved her. But his fears overwhelmed his desires. He finally stumbled over some woefully inadequate words.

"With a baby on the way, perhaps we...uh...maybe we should talk about—" He swallowed his panic as it tried to rob him of his ability to speak. "Uh...consider maybe living together."

This latest slap was more than Jean could handle. She jumped up from the sofa and glared at him for a moment. She lashed out at him, partly from anger and partly because she was very fearful of what the future held, of how she would be able to cope on her own.

"You just assumed I'd pack up and move to Chicago with you without any word about a commitment? That I'd simply abandon my own life and go with you until..." She searched for the right words, momentarily at a loss as her anger took precedence over her hurt. "Until you got tired of me? Until you decided that I'd manipulated you, too, and you'd had enough and wanted out?"

Then the reality hit her. That was what his evaluation report had been about. It was the final blow.

"And your report to Matt...was that your way of making sure you had control? That you would get what you wanted without any regard for me or my—"

She saw the confusion flash across his face, an expression that stopped her in midsentence and left her as confused as he looked.

His voice contained a combination of bewilderment and anger. "What the hell are you talking about? What does my report have to do with you being pregnant and my wanting to be involved with raising our child...and being with you?"

"I read the report. It very clearly stated your recommendation to eliminate my job! That would certainly put me in a position where I didn't have a lot of choices about career, especially trying to find a new job and telling a prospective employer that I'll be needing maternity leave in a few more months. That's not a situation most prospective employers want to embrace.''

A flash of understanding hit him. It all became clear. He now suddenly realized what she was talking about. He composed himself in an attempt to project a calm and collected outer manner. He maintained a soft and soothing tone of voice. ''You didn't read the entire report? You only read about half of the first page.'' The words were said as much to himself as they were to her. He looked up, extending a questioning gaze. ''Isn't that correct?''

All of the fight drained out of her. The events had taken a strange and totally unexpected turn. Her anger once again dissolved into a deep fear. She felt as if she was on an emotional roller-coaster and couldn't make it stop. ''Uh…well, I haven't studied the entire report…not in depth.''

''The entire report?'' He shook his head and allowed a hint of a smile to pull at the corners of his mouth. ''As I said, you didn't read beyond the middle of page one.'' He grabbed her hand and pulled her on to the sofa next to him.

''Had you read the entire report you would have seen that I recommended the elimination of the position of personnel manager because I recommended the change-over of the personnel department to a human resources department in line with other businesses of the same size as Jarvis Custom Furniture. I made suggestions for several changes, but none of them were due to any inadequacy on your part. They related to the way so many miscellaneous functions and problems seemed to be dumped on you, things that did not belong in a human resources department. I stated that the position of the personnel manager should be replaced with a new position that carried the title of Director Of Human Resources which should include an increase in salary.''

Jean sat in stunned silence as she tried to assimilate what he had said. ''I...I feel so foolish...I didn't read all...with everything else that's happened I just assumed...'' She looked up at him, searching his eyes for the compassion and understanding she so desperately needed.

He put his arm around her and pulled her close to him. ''I do understand.''

Ry pushed ahead with the rest of what he had to say before he lost his nerve again. ''And as far as living together...I didn't mean to imply that I thought you should quit your job, pick up your life and take it to Chicago especially since I had just recommended a raise and promotion for you. I can work out some way to move my corporate headquarters to Seattle. I've recently purchased a small public relations firm here and I think I can incorporate my other business interests into that location without too much of a problem.''

What had been anger, panic and fear several minutes ago had turned to embarrassment as she realized her erroneous assumption, then those feelings gave way to a growing exhilaration and finally culminated in an overwhelming excitement. It felt as if the weight of the world had suddenly been lifted from her shoulders. Everything would be okay after all. Then her new found euphoria found a dark cloud to dampen the moment.

The words were difficult for her, but they had to be said. There couldn't be any further misconceptions lingering to cause future problems. ''I don't want you to stay simply because you feel it's your responsibility. You've never once mentioned the word love to me. If we don't have the basis of a loving relationship where the baby will have a happy home, then I want you to leave now. I don't want a relationship built on nothing more than your feeling obligated to take responsibility. Having you *like* me isn't enough."

There—she had finally said it. She had told him she needed to know how he felt. She needed an all-out commitment. Having him say he was willing to accept responsibility was not enough.

Ry took a deep breath. He could not dance around it any longer. He wrapped her in his embrace. "You and the baby are the most important things in my life, far more important than any business deal I've signed or financial goal I've set for myself. I...I love you, Jean...I love you very much. I want us to be married as soon as possible. I want us to be a family—a real family."

The tears filled her eyes, but this time they were tears of joy. They were the words she had longed to hear, but feared she never would. She saw the seriousness in his eyes and the open love there for anyone to see, a love that was no longer hidden.

There was one last question, one last point to clarify. "Are you sure, Ry? Really sure?"

"Yes..." He stroked her hair and placed a tender kiss on her lips. "I've wanted to tell you for so long, but I've been so afraid—afraid of the commitment...the whole thing. But what scared me even more was the thought of losing you." He held her tight as the emotional wave washed over him. "The possibility of losing you put everything in proper perspective for me. It showed me how unimportant my inner fears were. It showed me how wrong I've been to let the demons of the past control my present when I should have been searching for the joys of the future."

"Oh, Ry...I've been so frightened. I didn't know what

to do. All I knew was that I loved you so much, was pregnant with your child and you had rejected me and the baby. Then when I saw the first page of your report…well…''

''I'm so sorry, Jean. I seem to be saying that a lot lately, but I mean it. That was a terrible thing I did to you even though it wasn't my intention. I want to spend the rest of my life making it up to you.'' He held her tightly. He had finally been able to tell her he loved her and she had returned that love. ''I want us to get married next week,'' he kissed her on the cheek, ''or sooner if it's possible. I'll start my attorney on the ramifications of moving my company to Seattle and we'll look for a house to buy.''

''Are you sure, Ry? Really sure?''

''I've never been so sure of anything in my life.''

Her heart soared as the love she felt for him filled every corner of her existence. A man she loved more than she thought possible, a home and a real family…it was everything she had ever wanted.

''Oh, Ry…I love you so much. Yes, I'll marry you. Whenever you want and wherever you want.''

He captured her mouth with a kiss that conveyed all the love that had been stored inside him. For the first time in his life he had someone to give that love to, someone that fulfilled his life. And they were going to have a baby, a new life created from their love. He had never been happier.

Epilogue

Ry pulled into the garage of the large house on Bainbridge Island that overlooked the bay with the Seattle skyline in the background. Even though they had been married for six months, it was only three months ago that they found the perfect house. There was still some landscaping to do and a couple of rooms to furnish yet, but for the most part they were settled and comfortable in their new home. He entered from the garage through the utility room, then into the kitchen.

He looked around and when he didn't see anyone, he called out. "Jean? Where are you?"

Her voice called back to him. "I'm in the den."

A moment later he pulled her into his arms and kissed her, a loving kiss that spoke of contentment and happiness. "What did the doctor say?"

"The doctor says everything is fine." She pointed to

the large gift-wrapped package in the middle of the floor. "I have a present for you."

"A present for me? What's the occasion?"

"Oh, let's just say it's because I love you."

"I love you, too, Mrs. Collier." He placed his hand on her burgeoning belly. "So much has happened. It took us all of three days to get married, then we found this house and now in a couple more months we'll have a new life to share our love with. I've never been happier."

She grinned at him, a smile that spoke of some hidden knowledge she wasn't sharing. "Open your present."

Ry studied the package for a moment, then carefully unwrapped the ribbon. Next he took off the wrapping paper. As soon as he saw the contents of the box he stopped. The magnitude of the event washed over him. He looked at Jean and saw the love in her eyes. He pulled her into his arms. The love he felt for her swelled inside him until there wasn't room for anything else.

"I can't believe this...you bought me a train. After twenty-four years I finally have my train."

"I thought it would be something you could share with our son."

He felt his eyes widen in shock. His words came out as a soft whisper. "Our son? Our baby will be a boy?"

"Yes, the tests confirmed it today. We're having a boy."

Ry held her tightly, his words barely audible. "A son..."

"I love you, Ry."

"Even though we're married, just seeing you still takes my breath away." He placed a loving kiss on her lips. "I love you so much. I can't imagine what the rest of my life would be like without you as part of it."

"You'll never have a chance to find out because I intend to spend the rest of my life with you."

* * * * *

Your opinion is important to us! Please take a few moments to share your thoughts with us about your experiences with Harlequin and Silhouette books. Your comments will be very useful in ensuring that we deliver books you love to read. *Please take a few minutes to complete the questionnaire, then send it to us at the address below.*

Send your completed questionnaires to:
Harlequin/Silhouette Reader Survey, P.O. Box 9046, Buffalo, NY 14269-9046

1. As you may know, there are many different lines under the Harlequin and Silhouette brands. Each of the lines is listed below. Please check the box that most represents your reading habit for each line.

Line	Currently read this line	Do not read this line	Not sure if I read this line
Harlequin American Romance	☐	☐	☐
Harlequin Duets	☐	☐	☐
Harlequin Romance	☐	☐	☐
Harlequin Historicals	☐	☐	☐
Harlequin Superromance	☐	☐	☐
Harlequin Intrigue	☐	☐	☐
Harlequin Presents	☐	☐	☐
Harlequin Temptation	☐	☐	☐
Harlequin Blaze	☐	☐	☐
Silhouette Special Edition	☐	☐	☐
Silhouette Romance	☐	☐	☐
Silhouette Intimate Moments	☐	☐	☐
Silhouette Desire	☐	☐	☐

2. Which of the following best describes why you bought *this book?* One answer only, please.

the picture on the cover	☐	the title	☐
the author	☐	the line is one I read often	☐
part of a miniseries	☐	saw an ad in another book	☐
saw an ad in a magazine/newsletter	☐	a friend told me about it	☐
I borrowed/was given this book	☐	other: _____	☐

3. Where did you buy *this book?* One answer only, please.

at Barnes & Noble	☐	at a grocery store	☐
at Waldenbooks	☐	at a drugstore	☐
at Borders	☐	on eHarlequin.com Web site	☐
at another bookstore	☐	from another Web site	☐
at Wal-Mart	☐	Harlequin/Silhouette Reader	☐
at Target	☐	Service/through the mail	
at Kmart	☐	used books from anywhere	☐
at another department store or mass merchandiser	☐	I borrowed/was given this book	☐

4. On average, how many Harlequin and Silhouette books do you buy at one time?

I buy _____ books at one time ☐
I rarely buy a book ☐

MRQ403SD-1A

5. How many times per month do you shop for any *Harlequin and/or Silhouette* books?
One answer only, please.

1 or more times a week	❑	a few times per year	❑
1 to 3 times per month	❑	less often than once a year	❑
1 to 2 times every 3 months	❑	never	❑

6. When you think of your ideal heroine, which *one* statement describes her the best?
One answer only, please.

She's a woman who is strong-willed		She's a desirable woman	❑
She's a woman who is needed by others	❑	She's a powerful woman	❑
She's a woman who is taken care of	❑	She's a passionate woman	❑
She's an adventurous woman		She's a sensitive woman	❑

7. The following statements describe types or genres of books that you may be
interested in reading. Pick *up to 2 types* of books that you are most interested in.

I like to read about truly romantic relationships ❑
I like to read stories that are sexy romances ❑
I like to read romantic comedies ❑
I like to read a romantic mystery/suspense ❑
I like to read about romantic adventures ❑
I like to read romance stories that involve family ❑
I like to read about a romance in times or places that I have never seen ❑
Other: _____ ❑

*The following questions help us to group your answers with those readers who are
similar to you. Your answers will remain confidential.*

8. Please record your year of birth below.
19 ____

9. What is your marital status?
single ❑   married ❑   common-law ❑   widowed ❑
divorced/separated ❑

10. Do you have children 18 years of age or younger currently living at home?
yes ❑   no ❑

11. Which of the following best describes your employment status?
employed full-time or part-time ❑   homemaker ❑   student ❑
retired ❑   unemployed ❑

12. Do you have access to the Internet from either home or work?
yes ❑   no ❑

13. Have you ever visited eHarlequin.com?
yes ❑   no ❑

14. What state do you live in?
_____

15. Are you a member of Harlequin/Silhouette Reader Service?
yes ❑   Account # _____   no ❑   MRQ403SD-1B

COMING NEXT MONTH

#1543 WITH PRIVATE EYES—Eileen Wilks
Dynasties: The Barones
Socialite Claudia Barone *insisted* on helping investigate the attempted sabotage of her family's business. But detective Ethan Mallory had a hard head to match his hard body. He always worked on his own....he didn't need the sexy sophisticate on the case. What he *wanted*...well, that was another matter!

#1544 BABY, YOU'RE MINE—Peggy Moreland
The Tanners of Texas
In one moment, Woodrow Tanner changed Dr. Elizabeth Montgomery's life. The gruff-yet-sexy rancher had come bearing news of her estranged sister's death—and the existence of Elizabeth's baby niece. Even as Elizabeth tried to accept this startling news, she couldn't help but crave Woodrow's consoling embrace....

#1545 WILD IN THE FIELD—Jennifer Greene
The Lavender Trilogy
Like the fields of lavender growing outside her window, Camille Campbell looked sweet and delicate, but could thrive even in the harshest conditions. Divorced dad and love-wary neighbor Pete MacDougal found in Camille a kindred soul...whose body could elicit in him the most amazing feelings....

#1546 CINDERELLA'S CHRISTMAS AFFAIR—Katherine Garbera
King of Hearts
Brawny businessman Tad Randolph promised his parents he'd be married with children before Christmas—and cool-as-ice executive CJ Terrance was the perfect partner for his pretend wedding and baby-making scheme. But soon Tad realized she was more fire than ice...and found himself wishing CJ shared more than just his bed!

#1547 ENTANGLED WITH A TEXAN—Sara Orwig
Texas Cattleman's Club: The Stolen Baby
A certain sexy rancher was the stuff of fantasies for baby store clerk Marissa Wilder. So when David Sorrenson showed up needing Marissa's help, she quickly agreed to be a temporary live-in nanny for the mystery baby David was caring for. But could she convince her fantasy man to care for *her*, as well?

#1548 AWAKENING BEAUTY—Amy J. Fetzer
There was more to dowdy bookseller Lane Douglas than met the eye...and Tyler McKay was determined to find out her secrets. Resisting the magnetic millionaire was difficult for Lane, but she vowed to keep her identity under wraps...even as her heart and body threatened to betray her.

SDCNM1003